"Grace, honey."

Jack smoothed her hair with slow, gentle strokes. "Reckon you're feeling about as low as anyone can get about now. But for what it's worth to you, I'm here. And I'm not leaving until you feel better."

"You d-don't have to be nice to me, you know." Grace hiccupped. "I just tried to shoot you dead."

"Yeah, I know." His thumb stopped a stream of tears and wiped them away. "I'm not real happy about that, but I guess I'll have to forget about it for now."

"Stay with me tonight," she whispered.

"Don't think you could keep me away."

* * *

The Lawman's Redemption
Harlequin® Historical #1003—August 2010

Author Note

If you've read a few of my books by now, you'll know I love to have my characters rub elbows with true historical figures from the Old West.

The Lawman's Redemption is no different. Jack Hollister wraps up a trilogy of stories beginning with *The Cattleman's Unsuitable Wife* and "The Cattleman's Christmas Bride" in *Cowboy Christmas,* both released last year. In this book, he clashes with Tom "Black Jack" Ketchum, an infamous outlaw who really holed up in New Mexico Territory and met his demise much as I depicted in the book.

Of course, few men have left their mark upon a community as strongly as Paris Gibson did in Great Falls, when Montana was a fledgling territory. His reputation and influence can still be seen today.

Lastly, Jack wrangles with one of the most intriguing villains I've ever written. Louis David Riel considered himself a divinely chosen leader and prophet of the Métis people in Canada. He was indeed exiled in the United States for a time and finally succumbed to charges of treason and was executed. Ironically, today he is considered a hero. A man who did what he did for the freedom of his people.

With that, I present to you *The Lawman's Redemption*.

The Lawman's Redemption

PAM CROOKS

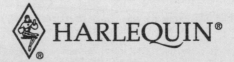

HARLEQUIN®

TORONTO • NEW YORK • LONDON
AMSTERDAM • PARIS • SYDNEY • HAMBURG
STOCKHOLM • ATHENS • TOKYO • MILAN • MADRID
PRAGUE • WARSAW • BUDAPEST • AUCKLAND

Recycling programs
for this product may
not exist in your area.

ISBN-13: 978-0-373-29603-3

THE LAWMAN'S REDEMPTION

Copyright © 2010 by Pam Crooks

This edition published by arrangement with Harlequin Books S.A.

For questions and comments about the quality of this book please contact us at Customer_eCare@Harlequin.ca.

www.eHarlequin.com

Printed in U.S.A.

Praise for Pam Crooks

The Cattleman's Unsuitable Wife

"The battle between sheepherders and cattlemen forms the compelling backdrop of Crooks's realistic Western and provides a natural conflict between the strong-willed hero and heroine and a plotline to hold readers enthralled."
—*RT Book Reviews*

Kidnapped by the Cowboy

"Crooks's solid understanding of the West and human nature adds another dimension to a story rife with misunderstandings, guilt and adventure."
—*RT Book Reviews*

Untamed Cowboy

"With its intense Western flavor, suspense and strong, realistic characters, this novel is vintage Crooks."
—*RT Book Reviews*

"I was captivated from the very first page of *Untamed Cowboy*. Although the book's conclusion was wonderfully satisfying, I was disappointed to see this end. Pam Crooks's *Untamed Cowboy* is one of the best historical Westerns I've read—ever!"
—*Romance Reader at Heart*

Wanted!

"With her signature talent for setting the gritty reality of the West alongside a sweet, tender romance, Crooks entertains with a tale that satisfies as it warms the heart."
—*RT Book Reviews*

"*Wanted!* was a superior historical Western. Fast-paced, realistic characters and a very well put-together story put this at the top of the genre. Pam Crooks has been a longtime favorite and *Wanted!* was no exception."
—*The Best Reviews*

The Mercenary's Kiss

Nominated for Best Historical K.I.S.S. Hero by *RT Book Reviews*

"With its nonstop action and a hold-your-breath climax, Crooks's story is unforgettable. She speaks to every woman's heart... The power that comes from the pages of this book enthralls."
—*RT Book Reviews*

To the Fillies at Petticoats & Pistols:
Kate Bridges, Linda Broday, Mary Connealy, Karen Kay,
Stacey Kayne, Elizabeth Lane, Patricia Potter,
Charlene Sands and Cheryl St.John.

Thank you for the laughs, the successes and your
dedication to Western romance.

But most of all, thank you for the sisterhood.

Available from Harlequin® Historical and
PAM CROOKS

Prologue

New Mexico Territory, 1883

Damned if life wasn't full of downright pathetic ironies.

Jack Ketchum drew in deep on his cigarette and pondered why it had to come to this. A son hunting down his own father. Kin exacting justice from kin.

Blood against blood.

He squinted through a swirl of slowly exhaled smoke. A grim blanket of sadness settled over his shoulders, weighing him down with regret. Until he reminded himself that Sam Ketchum needed saving from himself. And if Jack didn't save him, no one would.

He shivered and thought fleetingly of the hour. Had to be midnight, at least. Probably later. The air's chill had seeped into his bones, and he craved the warmth and comfort of the small apartment he kept in Colorado.

Unfortunately partaking in those comforts wasn't going to happen anytime soon. Comforts far different than the life his father had chosen. A life on the run. An outlaw's life. Hiding out somewhere deep in the rugged Sierra Grande Mountains, protected by a night so black, so thick, it seemed no posse could ever find him.

But Jack would. He had to. Or else it'd just be a matter of time until his father wound up dead.

Sam Ketchum would find it mildly amusing his only son had turned lawman and rode with men determined to arrest him and his brother, Tom "Black Jack" Ketchum. Along with their gang, the pair had made a reputation for themselves robbing trains, banks and anything else loaded with loot ripe for taking. For too long, their greed had hurt innocent people and ruined countless lives—including Jack's and the one woman who meant the world to him. His mother.

Like it or not, Sam would have to accept the time had come for it all to end.

Somehow.

Jack studied the glowing tip of his cigarette. The "somehow" part scared him, and the longer it took for Jack and the posse to track the gang down, the more likely it'd be the outlaw brothers would catch wind of it, then who knew which rock they'd hide under? Or where?

A new wave of resolve swelled through him, and

his glance shifted toward the fire burning low in the nearby camp. Around it, six men filled bedrolls—four of them lawmen like himself, the other two agents for the Colorado and Southern Railway Company. Heavily armed even in sleep, each one was as fiercely dedicated to enforcing the law as Jack.

Patience, he knew. He just needed patience to find his father and bring him in for his own good.

Jack's thighs protested his hunkered stance. Since his spell as night watch was just about up, he grasped his rifle and lifted the cigarette to his lips for a final drag, inhaling as he straightened.

Halfway to standing, a rock crunched behind him.

His every muscle coiled. But he kept moving, until he stood at full height.

He didn't turn around. Not yet. Instinct told him it wasn't an animal behind him, at least not one from the wild. Instead this creature stood on two legs, was likely armed, and judging from the stark silence, he was standing stock-still, watching Jack real close.

"You're Sam Ketchum's son, aren't you?" a low voice said.

The question surprised Jack. *Sam Ketchum's son.* Who out here on this mountain would know him like that?

He flicked the cigarette stub, sending it sailing in a neat arc into the rough buffalo grass. He tightened his grasp on his rifle and took his time answering.

"Who's asking?" he demanded finally.

"No one you know."

"Yet you know me."

Iron control kept Jack from turning to put a face to the voice in the darkness. He didn't know what he was up against, or what this man wanted from him. Mostly he didn't know if he'd live or die, shot in the back at any given moment....

"It seems I do know you, yes," the voice purred. "Better than you think."

"And you know my father, too."

"Quite well, as a matter of fact."

Jack's curiosity raged. The man's words carried a faint accent. French, maybe, but too slight to be native-born. Each word was refined, articulate. Cleverly taunting.

What was his association with Sam Ketchum? And why had he sought out Jack?

"You're looking for your father, aren't you?" the voice asked smoothly, reading Jack's thoughts. "You and your posse."

Jack's glance lifted toward the fire and the men sleeping around it, each oblivious to the stranger who had found them all on this desolate, unforgiving mountain in the middle of the night.

"Yes," Jack said.

"I know where he is."

Jack stilled. "How do you know?"

"I just do."

Suddenly impatient with the man's game, Jack swore, tossed his rifle to the ground and heard it land with a dull thud. He well realized the risk he took leaving himself unshucked, but the man had to know Jack wasn't a threat, not when the stranger had gone to great lengths to seek him out. Jack figured he came for one of two reasons: to help him or to hurt him.

He hoped it was the former.

He lifted his hands and half twisted to confront the stranger, to see a face and demand a name, but a snarled oath and the sharp snap of a jerked-back hammer convinced Jack of his mistake.

"Damn you, don't turn around," the voice growled.

"Where is he?" Jack demanded through his teeth. "Tell me where my father is."

The faint crunch of a boot heel on rocky ground warned him the stranger had taken a step back. One, then another. Jack's heart pounded from the very real possibility the stranger would disappear without revealing Sam Ketchum's whereabouts.

"There's a cave in a hill not far from the Cimarron. The base of Capulin Mountain, this side of Folsom," the voice rumbled. "Sam will be there, hiding out with Black Jack and the rest of the gang."

Hope soared inside Jack. A pathetic need to believe. To trust this man and all he claimed. "If you're lying, I swear—"

"They'll be there," the voice repeated coldly. "Waiting for the Fort Worth and Denver Express, due in two days' time."

Metal jangled softly against metal, and it took Jack a

moment to realize the sound came from saddle rigging. He whirled, his glance raking through the darkness to grasp the indistinct shape of a tall man with long hair leaping onto his mount, his arm encased in a heavily fringed jacket sleeve.

Then, before Jack could stop him, horse hooves rumbled, and the stranger was gone.

Only a fool would've attempted to ride down the mountain blinded by the night. Rocky trails so narrow, so winding, one misstep would send an unsuspecting horse hurtling over the steep edge into crippling oblivion, and then what would they have done?

It'd required every shred of Jack's patience to wait until the night lifted and dawn crept in. By the time it did, the posse was up and ready to ride, daring to trust in the stranger's information, yet prepared for his betrayal, too. Who knew how far Sam and Black Jack would go to keep the law off their trail? Including Sam's own son?

But the stranger hadn't betrayed them, and they located the cave with unerring accuracy. Jack found it damned unsettling to hide in the brush to spy on the gang while they moved about their camp. Every glimpse of his father twisted like a knife deep in his belly.

For reasons Jack couldn't yet fathom, the stranger wanted Sam Ketchum set up for arrest. But for Jack, it was more important to keep his father from robbing yet another express train—and to end his life of crime forever.

"Getting late, Jack. If we don't move in on 'em now, we're going to lose our chance."

Sheriff Edward Farr headed up the posse, but he took sympathy on Jack's situation. He'd been more than patient, giving Jack the time he needed to prepare himself for what lay ahead.

"I know," Jack said, grim.

The lawman heaved a troubled sigh. "Things are likely to get ugly for your pa and uncle, but don't forget there's a woman in that gang, too."

"I haven't forgotten."

Bess Reilly, rumored to be as tough and ruthless as any man. But Jack figured if she committed a man's crime, she had to pay the price like one.

"I got a bad feeling about this, Jack. Real bad." Farr shifted, as if to settle the nerves squirming inside him.

Jack's stare locked on movement at the front of the cave. If Sam Ketchum could've heard their scheming, he never would've reappeared right then, his heavy gun belt strapped around his hips. His glance slid one way and then the other in careful inspection of his surroundings, and Jack knew what he had to do.

"I'm going in first," he said.

"Not alone, you're not," the lawman said in a rough whisper.

"Maybe I can get him to listen to me."

"He won't." The retort dripped with disgust. "You know he won't."

Jack didn't bother denying it, but he clutched his rifle and eased out of the brush. His father moseyed over to a stand of trees and began to unbutton the front of his pants.

Jack kept going. The muted rustle of cocked weapons assured him of six men's protection. He strode closer to the infamous Sam Ketchum, and suddenly, time fell away, and he was a little boy again, hungry for the love and attention he'd long been denied—

Except Sam Ketchum had always been a sorry excuse for a father, and wasn't it a hell of a shame that it had to come to this? His own son sneaking up on him with a rifle pointed at his back while he took a leak?

Hell of a shame, all right. And Jack swallowed hard against the ugly truth. He didn't trust Sam Ketchum any farther than he could spit.

"Sorry to interrupt, old man, but there's a thing or two we need to talk about," he drawled.

The muscles in Sam's shoulders jerked. Jack kept a keen eye on those revolvers hanging in their holster, but his father merely finished with nature's call and set about refastening his pants.

"Well, now. Damned if it isn't my boy I'm hearin' behind me," Sam drawled back.

My boy. Jack's gut went tight.

"Fancy that," he said.

His father casually lifted his hands and turned to face him. Jack steeled himself against the familiarity of that thick moustache, those cheeks always in need of shaving.

"If I'd a-known you were comin' to call, I would've prepared a right proper welcome for you," Sam said.

"The hell you would."

"It's true."

"You're surrounded, just so you know."

Sam nodded once. Unaffected. "I figured."

"Tell the others to give up. We can end this without blood spilling."

"How did you find me?"

His father's voice had turned guttural, and Jack glimpsed the hard side of him. The ruthless part that earned him the reputation for being one of the most notorious outlaws in the territory.

"A friend of yours enlightened me," he said.

"Who?" he demanded sharply.

Jack lifted a shoulder in a careless shrug. "I don't know, and it doesn't matter, besides."

"It matters to me!"

"Someone wanted you found as much as I did. He did me a favor."

Sam's lip curled beneath the moustache. "A favor."

Impatience rolled through Jack. His father's arrest wasn't going to happen while they stood here, exercising their jaws, wasting valuable time and increasing the chances of detection by the rest of the gang.

"You're at the end of the line, old man," Jack said in

a terse voice. "Throw down your shooting irons. You're coming with us."

Sam eyed the tin star on Jack's coat with contempt. "Just 'cuz you're workin' for the law these days don't mean I'm gonna do what you tell me to do."

"Someone has to save your sorry ass."

"My ass don't need savin', boy," he snapped. "Ride out of here while you still can. And take that damn posse with you."

Jack's grip tightened on his rifle. "Can't do that."

A lethal, sober calm seemed to come over Sam. For long moments, he didn't move. "Then I got no choice but to do what I gotta do."

Jack's blood pounded, hard in his veins.

Lightning quick, Sam grabbed for his guns. "Now, Tom!"

And before Jack could fathom the signal, before he could anticipate his uncle tearing out of the shadows, a blaze of gunfire erupted in front of him, behind him, around him. A deafening explosion of vengeance and desperation, of law against the lawless, of hate and honor and determination...

But as if time moved in slow motion, Jack was aware of only his father and that he lifted and leveled his revolver. Of the hammer cocked back and the bullet catapulting toward him. Of the burn screaming across his cheek—

And because he was Sam Ketchum's son, capable of fury and vengeance, too, Jack reacted with his aim just as deadly, his hand moving split-second fast over the rifle, his heart cold against the way the bullet spun his father's body and threw him into the dirt.

As fast as it started, the gun battle ended. Sheriff Farr laid dead, alongside the rest of his posse, each of them victims to their dedication to the law. The Ketchum gang laid, too, scattered like rag dolls, paying the price for the wrongs they'd committed.

Only Black Jack managed to escape, leaving his brother behind to die at the hands of his son.

Jack lowered the rifle and held it loosely at his side. He strode toward his father. Face ashen, his shoulder shattered and blood-soaked, Sam struggled to breathe.

"Looks like you won, don't it, boy?" he rasped.

Jack didn't bother to explain it wasn't about winning or losing. Not anymore. Was it ever?

Dispassionate he stood—and waited for his father's time to come.

"I gotta know…who set me up," Sam said, the demand weak. Obsessive. "Find him for me, y'hear? Will you do that…for your ol' man, Jack?"

Jack had done what he set out to do.

But he'd failed. Failed in the worst way.

Then, Sam Ketchum's eyes rolled toward the back of his head, and his body sagged into death.

Blood ran in rivulets down Jack's cheek, but he was beyond feeling the pain. His hand lifted to the tin star he wore over his heart. For a moment, he cradled the badge in his palm and pondered all it stood for. Justice and honor and pride.

In grim finality, he tossed the star downward…where it landed tarnished on his father's chest.

Another pathetic irony in his life.

Cold to it, he walked away.

Chapter One

One year later

Jack Hollister pushed open the door to Margaret's Eatery, stomped his boots free of snow and stepped inside to a warmth that promised to thaw his bones. The fragrant aroma of roasting beef and strong coffee made coming back to Great Falls even sweeter.

The door swung open again, and his friend, Mick Vasco, strode in. He stomped his boots, too, then shut out the biting Montana wind with a firm latch.

"Damn, it's cold out there," he said unnecessarily.

Jack swept an automatic glance around the restaurant, but his feet were already moving toward his favorite table. The one against the big picture window, draped with red calico curtains.

Some habits just weren't meant to break.

Ever since his lawman days, he'd fancied a window that gave him a view. It was in his blood that way. A man on the inside who kept track of what was going on on the outside tended to have the advantage.

Mick pulled back the chair across from him and settled in. They took off their hats, hooked them on the back of their chairs and craned their necks to see if the best waitress in all of Great Falls was working her normal Sunday afternoon shift.

She was.

Jack's mother, Camille, was already heading toward them, a coffeepot in her hand. By the looks of her flushed cheeks and the wisps of gray curling along her temples, she'd spent the morning in the kitchen again, baking her juicy-on-your-tongue, made-to-perfection fruit pies in between serving customers hungry for Margaret Butterfield's—the restaurant's owner—hearty cooking.

"I expected you two back yesterday," she said quietly, upending a coffee cup. She began to pour. "Problems?"

Jack knew how she used to worry when he rode with the posse. This time would've been no different.

"Not unless you call the past six and a half days being a complete waste of our time a problem," Mick muttered.

"We followed up on some leads that didn't pan out," Jack said, eyeing the steam swirling over the rim of the cup. "Ran us late."

"Too bad." Camille made a sound of sympathy.

"About the leads, I mean." She tilted the pot over the cup Mick held ready and waiting.

Jack grunted. It had been a damned shame they hadn't found any sign of the gang involved in a complex embezzling scheme that stretched clear to Minnesota. Two men in particular who pulled off a train heist outside Great Falls that nearly cost Mick his life and scandalized the reputation of the woman he intended to marry.

"They're probably long gone by now anyway," Camille said. "You did the best you could."

Obviously his best hadn't been good enough.

And the itch was still there. Even now, months after he'd tossed aside his badge, walked away from his dream to be the best lawman this side of the Missouri and started his life over, a different man with a new name, the need for justice continued to burn in his blood.

"You're a cowboy now, Jack," she said in a faintly insistent voice. The one that revealed she knew what he was thinking and didn't approve. Because it scared her. "Not a lawman. Let the police do their job without you."

Jack sipped his coffee. Ignored the bite of fire on his tongue. Ignored *her*.

But he couldn't ignore Boone and his accomplice, not when they hovered within his every thought, fueling his need to find them, to even the score for the crimes they'd committed.

"Would you like the usual for dinner?" she asked finally, resigned.

He took the distraction she offered and ran with it. "Sounds good."

"Make it meatloaf for me," Mick put in. "With plenty of gravy."

"I'll make sure you get extra potatoes with it. Won't take but a minute," she said with her usual efficiency.

Jack's gaze followed her into the kitchen. She was still a fetching woman for her age, he mused. Slim-waisted and hardworking with an indomitable spirit that belied the difficult life she'd once led.

Yet Jack knew, too, as her only offspring, he was pretty much her sole reason for living. It'd crush her if anything happened to him. After all, it'd been just the two of them, surviving together, for so damn long.

He swallowed down a scowl. The old man had been too selfish to love her in the ways she deserved to be loved. Too stupid to realize their lives would've been so much different—*better*—if he had loved her.

Jack didn't amend the thought by adding himself into the mix. But he chased the bitterness down with a scalding gulp of coffee that took his mind off the past and brought him roughly back to reality.

"George will be here any minute," Mick said. "Let's order something for him to save time."

Through the picture window glass, Jack spied George Huys already walking down the snow-dusted boardwalk toward the eatery. As police chief for Great Falls, he led the posse in the hunt for the elusive train robbers and had stopped by his office to check for messages before dinner. Jack respected him as a lawman and a friend.

He rose. "I'll have Mom make up a plate for him."

"Bring the coffeepot back with you."

Jack nodded in acknowledgment and headed toward the kitchen. Along the way, he passed tables of diners dressed in their Sunday best, most of them in for dinner after a long morning of church services. The majority of faces were familiar, each one belonging to God-fearing folks that made Great Falls a wise place to live.

To escape.

Jack was glad this part of Montana was feeling more like home every day. He'd made friends, found a good job at the Wells Cattle Company, and enjoyed a deep friendship with Mick and his half brother, Trey Wells, both of whom made him feel like a part of their family instead of just another cowboy on their big, sprawling ranch.

For now, it was enough.

Jack added the police chief's order to their ticket and took the time to answer Margaret's questions on the posse's attempts in tracking down the outlaws. She had a vested interest in them being found, considering she'd been on the very train they robbed. Her attempt to thwart the crime had all but saved Mick's life and allowed him to escape with Allie Gibson, the victim of the gang's thievery. Margaret's disappointment that they continued to evade capture only strengthened Jack's resolve to hunt them down.

On his way out of the kitchen, he grabbed one of the coffeepots and headed back toward Mick.

"Timothy Richard, watch out!"

Jack abruptly halted just before a three-year-old catapulted to the floor in front of him, and he instinctively lifted the pot high and to the side to keep the rambunctious child from being splattered with hot liquid.

"I'm sorry, Jack." The boy's mother sounded exasperated. She bent to grasp her son's hand and right him again. "He never watches where he's going."

"No harm done, Sara," he said, though they both knew that if he'd tripped over the boy, injury from spilled coffee could've been serious.

"Haven't been able to teach him to walk instead of running all the time," his father added wryly and held Timmy in place with a firm hand on his shoulder. "We can't keep up with him most days."

Jack waved off their apologies with a commiserating chuckle, and the little family headed out of the restaurant at a more sedate pace.

In the next moment, Jack almost tripped again.

A black, deeply grained leather satchel stood angled in the aisle, likely knocked askew when clipped by the boy's foot. Frowning, Jack toed the expensive traveling bag closer to the owner's table and out of harm's way, sliding it next to a snow-wet shoe peeking out from beneath a deep blue hem.

Jack had always been partial to blue, and maybe that's

why this particular shade snagged his attention. A rich, vibrant blue, like a sun-drenched ocean.

Or maybe it was the way all that blue draped over a woman's slender lap as she perched on her chair, knees primly together, her head bent while she pored over her menu. Her concentration was so intense, had she even noticed her satchel was likely responsible for Timmy's fall?

Seemed she hadn't, and annoyed from it, Jack continued to his own table. He'd never seen her before, but then Margaret's Eatery was located near the Great Falls train station. Passengers came and went every day.

George Huys entered the restaurant on a swirl of cold air, and by the time he joined them, Jack had a third cup of coffee poured, with the first two topped off and steaming hot.

The police chief tossed a paper on the table and shrugged out of his coat. "Got a telegram while we were gone, Jack. Thought you might be interested."

"Yeah?" He sipped his brew. "What's it say?"

"Black Jack Ketchum is dead."

Jack slowly lowered his cup. He'd had no news of his uncle since the ambush in New Mexico Territory a year ago. That he remained alive until now, running from the law, shouldn't have surprised Jack.

But it did.

"He was blasted at close range trying to rob a train last week." George spoke matter-of-factly, with no sympathy for Jack's loss. "He got away wounded, but they caught him the next day, put him on trial and sentenced him to hang." The police chief grimaced, and for the first time, attempted to find the right words. "It wasn't pretty, but main thing is he's dead."

That old rush of pain reared up fast and fierce again, flooding Jack with the ugly reminder of how he'd been born the son of one outlaw and the nephew of another. Two brothers filled with greed and a taste for killing, who would always have had an appalling disregard for the law if the law hadn't triumphed over them first.

The curse of his bloodline, his need to survive and overcome the hate, had compelled Jack to rid himself of the Ketchum name and take his mother's maiden name of Hollister instead. Playing cowboy at the WCC, immersing himself in a new and different life, had helped, too. Some.

But damned how fate had a way of reminding him he was—and always would be—a Ketchum.

"Wish things could've been different for you." Mick's tone rumbled with understanding.

"Yeah, well…"

Jack's mind filled with a whole wagonload of spiteful comments he could make. Contemptuous slurs for the man who had fathered him. But like George Huys and Trey Wells, trusted friends who knew the truth of Jack's identity, Mick had heard them all before.

"Thanks," Jack said instead.

"Some men are just born for trouble," the police chief

said with a shake of his head. "Sam and Tom had a mean streak that just wouldn't quit."

Mean? Is that what it was when a father tried to kill his own son? When an uncle charged at his nephew with guns blazing, in hopes the two brothers could escape their crimes, only to commit more?

Jack hated that the pain could still hurt this much. But it did, and when in the hell was he going to get over it? Get on with his life like everyone else?

He could feel Mick and George watching him, and he angled his head to escape their sympathy. Several tables away, his glance stumbled onto the woman dressed in blue.

And latched on.

She was pure perfection in that high-society dress of hers. Trimmed with a black collar that looked like fur, fitted at the waist and shaped to her full breasts, she made a sight that made a man forget.

Perfection. Pure and simple.

God knew Jack needed some of that in his life when his own was just about as imperfect as it could be. The woman made staring a pleasure, compelled Jack to forget his manners and just keep on looking.

She was oblivious to him and most everyone else in the restaurant. Her menu engrossed her as she moved a fingertip precisely across the page, her finely shaped brows puckered in concentration as she read every word.

"Dinner's coming."

Mick's announcement broke Jack of his staring, and he spied his mother walking toward them, two hot plates balanced on her left arm and a third in her right hand. In unison, they shuffled their cups to give her room to serve them, and then eyed their meals in blatant appreciation.

"Anything else I can get you boys?" she asked.

"We're fine if you let us keep the coffeepot," George said, reaching to refill his cup. "Can't seem to get warm just yet."

"Go right ahead. There's more on the stove if you need it."

She bustled off again, and they dug in. Jack conceded a good hot meal and plenty of black brew was all he needed to feel human again. By the time they finished massive portions of whortleberry pie for dessert, the pot was empty.

"I'll get another one," Jack said, rose and retraced his steps to the kitchen. On the way back, he noticed the woman in blue waving her fingers to get his attention.

"Excuse me, sir," she said in a voice as soft as thistledown. "Are we to pour our own coffee here?"

Clearly the notion was foreign to her. As pampered as she looked, Jack wondered if she'd ever served anyone a meal before. Or made her own coffee.

"Not as a rule," he said. Of course, her eyes were blue. As blue as blue could be. Even bluer than her dress, and he had to work hard to keep from falling into that blue,

blue abyss. He cleared his throat. "The restaurant's busy, that's all."

"I see."

Appearing distracted, she blinked up at him. Jack felt acutely aware of how rough and trail-worn he must look to her. She wouldn't know he'd just spent the past week riding all over Montana Territory on a grueling manhunt.

Yet her gaze held a little too long, and, he knew then, what held her transfixed. The gift his father had given him. The permanent reminder of how Sam Ketchum would rather see him dead than be captured by the law.

He hated the scar on his cheek.

And from the way the woman averted her eyes, she didn't think much of it, either.

Jack set his teeth. She might be a vision of pure blue perfection, but he wasn't some sort of disfigured monster, no matter what she might think.

It became imperative that he prove it. Might be he just needed to show her a little old-fashioned hospitality, too.

"Let me fill your cup for you, ma'am," he drawled with exaggerated courtesy and righted her cup before she could refuse. "Coffee doesn't get any better than it is right here at Margaret's Eatery."

"Is that so?" She watched the steaming liquid rise closer to the rim, as if she preferred to avoid looking at him. Or his scar.

"It is, it is."

"Thank you, sir."

Her politeness touched a chord inside him. When before had a female called him "sir"? He couldn't step away from her if he wanted.

Which he didn't.

"Cream? Sugar?" he asked, stalling.

"I'll take it from here, Jack, thank you." His mother nudged him aside with a harried smile and complete attention for her customer. She scooped up the woman's finished dinner plate and utensils. "Would you like to order dessert now, ma'am?"

Jack knew when an opportunity had been taken from him, and he had no choice but to leave and let his mother do her job. He returned to his table, coffeepot still in hand, and found Mick highly amused from his efforts.

"Since when did you turn into such a fine waitress, Jack?" he snorted.

"Guess he's been hiding his apron from us all this time," George deadpanned.

Jack frowned. "She wanted coffee, that's all."

"Sure she did."

"Yessirree."

He turned testy from their teasing. Did they think she was too perfect for him?

Because, most likely, she was.

Jack scowled at their guffawing, tossed down a wad of bills for their meals and left.

Chapter Two

Grace Reilly stood outside Margaret's Eatery and warred with indecision on what to do next. A gust of wind blew right through her, and she shivered, quickly pulling the collar of her coat closer to her chin.

She had to find Allethaire, her best friend. Allethaire was in deep trouble, but then, so was Grace if she couldn't save the Ladies Literary Aid Society from the scandal she'd left behind in Minneapolis. The precious funds the ladies had raised to build a grand library had apparently been embezzled, then found days later in Allethaire's luggage, and *then*, stolen right out from under her nose, all in the shortest breadth of time.

Allethaire needed Grace, and Grace needed Allethaire. They needed each other to get the Society's money back and save both their reputations.

As if finding Allethaire wasn't enough, she needed

to find her younger half brother, too. Carl, whose last wire demanded that she come to Montana Territory as soon as she could. His cryptic message didn't give any details as to *why*, but Grace could only assume he was in trouble.

Again.

It had been a puzzling coincidence how both Allethaire and Carl needed her at the same time here in Great Falls. But it proved to be an important coincidence, too, reinforcing her belief that the decision to travel all the way from Minneapolis—alone—to this rough and barely civilized territory was the right thing to do.

Except she had no idea where Allethaire was. At least, not for sure. Since the night her friend had secretly fled Minneapolis under the threat of embezzlement charges, Grace hadn't heard a single word from her.

But she knew Allethaire well enough to believe in her innocence and to know she would run straight to her father for help. The powerful Paris Gibson was one of Great Falls' town leaders. So it made sense that Grace should seek him out first. Surely he'd know where his daughter was?

Grace shivered again and stepped back into the shelter of Margaret's Eatery, out of the wind. She kept a tight hold on the handle of her black walrus traveling bag, heavy from the precious files inside. Papers that would help save Allethaire.

Grace battled a flare of annoyance that Carl hadn't

met her at the train station, but instead left her to fend for herself in this unfamiliar town. Wasn't that just like him? To plead for her to come and then act as if he didn't care when she did?

Sighing, she slid her gaze down one side of the dirt street, then up the other and wondered if Great Falls was always so deserted on a Sunday afternoon. The restaurant had emptied of its customers and would be closing soon. She had Paris's address—thanks to Camille, the helpful waitress—but no way to get there.

Grace was accustomed to cabs running all day every day in Minneapolis, but clearly Great Falls had no such convenience. Now she'd have to find someone to drive her, even though she didn't know a soul, and never mind the rest of her baggage was still at the train station waiting to be claimed. Or that dusk would be falling soon. Or that it had started to snow—soft, quiet little flakes that began to gather.

And she had no place yet to stay the night.

A disconcerting wave of panic rolled through her belly, until she noticed a light shining through a window across the street. A business of some sort, and it became something to focus on. Direction. A possible avenue for help.

Hefting her satchel, she stepped away from the restaurant, onto the boardwalk. Her eyes watered from the cold, and she narrowed them to decipher tiny letters on that window.

PLOCEI

POLCIE
POLICE!

Any officer at the Great Falls Police Station would know Paris Gibson. They'd likely know if Allethaire was with him. They'd know where he lived, or at least how to find him. That's what policemen did. They found people.

Grace strode forward onto the snowy street in relief.

Suddenly horrified, she froze in midstep.

No. Oh, no. She couldn't go to the police. What if they knew about the accusations against Allethaire? It wouldn't matter how influential her father was, they'd still want to *arrest* her. In fact, they could be looking for her at this very minute, and if they found her, they'd throw her in *jail*, and Grace didn't *dare* go over to that stupid police station.

She retreated backward to the boardwalk, but before she could turn around and make a hasty run to the shelter of the restaurant, she knocked into something tall. Something solid.

She whirled and threw her head back in surprise. Her mind recoiled from the savage stranger before her. An involuntary yelp leaped from her throat.

Beneath a filthy flat-brimmed hat, his black hair straggled past his shoulders, and his cheeks were days overdue for shaving. A strong, unclean smell clung to him—a vile blend of horse, wood smoke and unwashed skin. Dark, fierce-looking, he reminded her of the devil himself....

Lucifer could claim his eyes. Black as ink, remote, fathomless. Shadowed and ominous under the brim, they watched her, as if they bided their time to snatch her up. To devour and conquer and force her to sin.

"You look lost," he said.

His voice didn't match his appearance. Low and smooth, his words sounded vaguely French.

Surprisingly civilized.

"I'm not lost," she said quickly and angled herself away to step around him.

He angled himself, too. Stopping her.

"You're new in town, aren't you?" he asked.

"Yes," she said carefully. Had it been so obvious?

"Is there something you're looking for? Someone you need to see?"

Despite his concern, she didn't trust him. No matter that every fiber of her being wanted to, that someone less prejudiced and more open-minded wouldn't care how the man looked like an unkempt savage or that he had an apparent willingness to help her.

Grace had learned from years back in her childhood how her instincts were hers and hers alone. So many times, they helped her survive when she felt too overwhelmed, too vulnerable, to go on.

And now was one time when she had to be strong.

Is there something you're looking for? Someone you need to see?

The words pounded in her head.

"No one," she lied.

"And yet you arrived here alone."

She stilled. Her brain scrambled to lie again. "How do you know I'm alone? Why, I—"

"Because I saw you when you arrived. There was no one with you on the train. No one to meet your arrival, either."

She blinked up at him.

"And your baggage is still waiting at the depot."

Her heart began to pound. He knew all about her. Because he'd been watching her. Waiting for her to finish her dinner and leave Margaret's Eatery. Alone.

Her alarm growing, she stepped back again. "I was just on my way to the police station," she said firmly. The officers needed to know that this, this *riffraff* had been spying on her when he had no right to do so. "If you'll excuse me, I'll continue on my way."

"You've come to see Allethaire, haven't you?"

The words purred their way through the air, jolting her with their chilling accuracy. Grace stood frozen, staring at him.

"How do you know about her?" she demanded hoarsely.

Allethaire would never associate with a man like him. Never. She'd always surrounded herself with society's elite. Community leaders. Honest and upright townspeople who were her friends, and her father's friends.

Never a savage.

"I just do," he said.

A horrible dread rose up inside her. "Who are you?"

"A friend," he purred again.

"No." Grace shook her head. "I don't believe you."

He cocked his head, as if amused by her defiance. "Would you like me to take you to her?"

A new round of terror gripped Grace. A terrible fear that he'd found Allethaire, hurt her, kept her against her will.

It could happen, she knew. This harsh, godforsaken, barely settled piece of Montana would make it easy to hide her away, far and deep into the wilderness so no one could find her. Until it was too late.

"What have you done with her?" she choked. "Where is she?"

The savage gripped her elbow. But his smile never wavered. "I'll take you to her."

"No." She yanked against his hold. "Let go of me."

Grace shot a frantic look toward Margaret's Eatery, but the windows were dark now. The restaurant had closed. The boardwalks and streets were deserted, too, and the police station seemed so terribly far away.

"You're very beautiful, Grace. Do you know that?"

He tugged her toward a narrow path that ran between the eatery and a hardware store. A shadow-filled alley that would chew her up and swallow her whole.

Grace knew she couldn't go there. No good would come of it if she did. She shrieked and dug her heels in, but they just skidded and slid in the gathering snow. She stumbled, writhed, and fought; the savage merely tightened his grip.

She was no match for his strength, yet she fought all the harder, throwing her weight away from him. Her satchel dropped with a heavy thud; she clenched her fist and pounded his body with awkward, frenzied blows. His thick fringed coat simply muffled them.

Her terror grew. "Damn you, let me go. Who are you? Why are you doing this to me?"

His coldhearted silence unnerved her, but it was the cunning resolve in his stride that unnerved her more. He dragged her deeper into the alley, past barrels of trash and stacks of empty crates, toward a lone horse tethered to a tree.

Grace vowed she'd not make it easy for him to take her away. She'd fight and kick and scream—

Someone stepped out from behind the restaurant. A man. Tall, broad, lean. Silhouetted in the mouth of the alley with his feet spread and his body positioned between them and the horse.

Another scream bubbled in Grace's throat. Dear God, she couldn't fight them both, these two men who conspired to kidnap her for reasons she couldn't in a million years fathom.

"Reckon the lady doesn't want to go wherever you're taking her," he said.

Grace couldn't breathe, could barely think, but her brain registered the low drawl as familiar.

The stranger tensed. "She's lost, that's all."

"No!" She strained against him all over again. "I'm not!"

"She asked me to help her." Straight teeth gleamed, an arrogant smile which curved the stranger's lips. Never, Grace noted, did he take his eyes off the other man. "Women. Always fickle, aren't they?"

Fickle? *Fickle?*

"Some, I suppose," the man said with a slight shrug. "But not this one." His arm lifted. His position shifted. In the dusky light surrounding him, an ominous revolver took shape. "And not now."

She almost wept. She remembered him from the restaurant. The scar on his cheek, the way he'd poured her coffee, exaggeratedly courteous and faintly teasing. Mostly the way his eyes had lingered over her face…

Jack, the helpful Camille had called him. *Jack.* And the sweet ache of hope coursed through Grace's blood.

"You'll save us all a heap of trouble if you let her go." Jack's voice hardened. "So do it easy and do it now."

For a moment, the savage-looking stranger didn't move. Didn't speak. Grace imagined him weighing his options, his abilities, and she held her breath for what he might and might not do.

Then, amazingly enough, he released her. "Of course." He stepped to the side, lifted his grimy hands to show compliance and turned to her. Again, that smile came, as dangerous as it was charming. "It seems we had an unfortunate misunderstanding. Forgive me, won't you?"

He would've been gallant if he hadn't been so vile. Disgust roiled in her belly.

"I have no intention of doing anything of the sort."

She moved to put more distance between them, her feet instinctively taking her closer to the protection of the revolver and the man who wielded it.

Jack met her coming. He kept his weapon's aim steady, his free hand reaching for her.

"Stay right there, mister," he ordered the stranger in a cold voice. "We're going to pay a little visit to the police. They're going to be real interested in why you—"

A violent push slammed into Grace's shoulder blades, and she catapulted into Jack with such force she couldn't think fast enough to avoid him. He swore at the sudden onslaught of her body, and they both grappled for balance.

In the blur of a single leap, the savage grabbed Jack next and hurled him sideways. His revolver's aim lost, Jack's arm hooked her waist to cushion their fall, twisting their bodies together as they toppled to the ground.

On the way down, Grace's head cracked against an empty crate, and stars burst before her eyes. Jack landed with a grunt, his muscular bulk thrown half-over, half-under her. The air whooshed from her lungs.

For a dazed moment, he consumed her senses. His heaviness, his warmth, his strength. The roughness of his coat, the husky rasp of his breath, his scent—a bold mix of leather, tobacco and brisk Montana cold.

But in the next, he spat a vehement oath that blazed fire in her ears. He untangled himself from her skirts and bolted to his feet.

"Stay right there," he ordered. "Y'hear me? Stay."

He swung toward the stranger fast making his escape and took off after him. Alarmed, Grace scrambled to sit up.

The restaurant's back door swung open wide. Bundled against the cold, Margaret Butterfield's matronly shape appeared.

"Ach!" She rushed out with a gasp. "What happened here?"

Another woman followed on her heels. Camille, the waitress. "Oh, you poor thing!"

Grace attempted to right her hat and managed with only minimal success. A careful probe with a fingertip found the tender spot on her head.

"I'm fine," she said, fearing it was only partially true.

"You've had the scare of your life." Camille bent to slip an arm around her and help her up. "How can you be fine?"

"Did someone attack you? Who? Why?" Margaret demanded, helping, too. She brushed snow off Grace's coat.

"I don't know," Grace said unsteadily. "I never saw

him before, but he tried to make me go with him. It was *awful*."

Camille enveloped her in a quick hug. "Of course, it was."

"Another man—Jack—went after him." Grace spoke around tears that refused to be quelled. "I don't know what I would've done if he—he hadn't come when he did."

"Jack Hollister?" Camille appeared taken aback. "My son?"

"He's smart as they come," Margaret said firmly, producing a handkerchief for Grace, who accepted it gratefully. "If the man who tried to hurt you has any sense at all, he'd know not to come around here again. Jack and the law will make sure he'll regret it."

Grace nodded and tried to take comfort in her words.

Until she met the troubled light in Camille's eyes.

And they both knew, no matter what Margaret said, the stranger would be back.

Chapter Three

Jack pulled up at the hitching post in front of Lindell's Boardinghouse, dismounted and whipped the reins into a tight knot. If only he could've done the same to the long-haired stranger's neck instead.

The no-good fool had gotten away, thanks to the close proximity of his horse and the advantage of a head start. Though Jack's chase had been respectably swift and hard-driven, the bastard had escaped into the hills, his tracks lost in the rough and rocky buffalo grass.

What his intentions were with the Lady in Blue, Jack couldn't imagine, but it had been clear by her struggles she was an innocent victim. At least, Jack had stumbled upon them in time to prevent her from being snatched away, damn it. Once he'd lost sight of the man and was forced to admit defeat, he hightailed it back to the restaurant. Not unexpectedly, the place had long since closed, and both Margaret and his mother were gone.

But he'd bet his last dime they knew something of the whereabouts of the Lady in Blue.

The dark, swollen clouds ushered dusk in early, and the boardinghouse's windows glowed with light. Jack leaped up the stairs, removed his Stetson and slapped the brim against his thigh. Snow scattered over the porch.

Before he could clasp the knob and let himself in, the door swung open.

"Finally, Jack!" his mother said. "I was worried about you."

A corner of his mouth lifted. "So what else is new?"

He chucked her under the chin, strode inside and met the warmth from a crackling fire. The hushed quiet indicated the boarders had already retired to their rooms for the night.

She closed the door after him. "Any luck?"

"None." His mood returned to grim. He hung his coat on a brass hook, added his hat, but left his holster of Colts strapped on. He turned toward her. "Do you know anything?"

"Unfortunately not. Margaret and I were just closing up the restaurant when we heard the commotion. We missed the whole thing."

Alarm flared inside him. "You don't know where she went then?"

Her head cocked. A knowing glint sparkled in her eyes. "Who?"

"The Lady in Blue."

"Ah." She nodded once. "Grace."

Jack's heart turned over. Grace. Funny how just knowing her name affected him. A perfect name for a woman who was all beauty, perfection and…grace.

"Grace Reilly," his mother added.

"And?" He held his breath.

"She's here."

The news startled him. "Here?" Not with friends? Family? Or at a hotel? He pointed to the floor. "As in *right* here?"

"No." Camille smiled and pointed a finger toward the ceiling. "As in up there."

His glance lifted toward the stairwell. The hallway lined with four doors. She was so close.

Right here. Only footsteps away.

Anticipation flared in his blood. "I need to talk to her."

"Later, Jack," Camille said firmly. "She's resting. Poor thing was still shaking when I gave her a room."

He grimaced. Hell of an ordeal for anyone to go through, but it had to be worse for a woman alone with no means to defend herself.

Curiosity about her rolled through him—who she was, why she was here. Why she had no one with her. And why the stranger would want to kidnap her.

At least she was settled in for the night. Safe, most of all.

"Thanks for taking care of her," he said and meant it.

"Of course. How could I have done anything else?"

Camille longed to have her own house someday. Reasonable rent at Lindell's allowed her to board for as long as she needed to, and in the time she'd been there, she could all but run the place. Now was one time when Jack was glad she could.

She regarded him. "I didn't know you were still in town. I thought you would have headed back to the ranch after dinner."

He didn't tell her he delayed his return to inform her of Black Jack's death. Or that while he waited for her shift to end, he'd shoveled the walkways around the boardinghouse to make her life a little easier.

He didn't want to inflict the inevitable pain from hearing how justice had finally caught up with her brother-in-law just yet. She'd picked up the pieces of her life after Sam Ketchum's death. Reminding her of Black Jack would bring the turmoil back again.

The Lady in Blue—Grace, he corrected himself, Grace Reilly—concerned him more. Black Jack could wait.

"I had some unfinished business to take care of," he said instead.

If she was curious, she didn't show it. "Sit down. I'll get you some coffee. Are you by yourself?"

Jack's glance followed her as she strolled across the main floor into the kitchen. Watched her reach for a cup, then the hot pot on the stove. Without the apron she always wore while working at the restaurant, she looked more slender than usual.

"Yes," Jack said. "Mick rode on out to the ranch."

"He couldn't wait to see Allie, I'm sure." She smiled.

"It was burning a hole in him."

It burned something different through Jack. Envy. A longing so deep, so intense, his stomach hurt and his heart ached.

More and more often of late, he was haunted by how a man needed a woman to complete his life. Children, too. A family to make him whole and to give him a reason to keep living, day after day, year after year.

Jack had all but given up hope of finding a woman that could fill the hungry hole inside him. The perfect woman. One that wouldn't see the ugly scar on his face or care how it got there. A woman who would be unaffected by the Ketchum roots that would forever make him kin of outlaws.

"They're very fortunate to have found each other," she said softly.

"I know."

Jack heard the wistfulness in her tone. Knew she felt the same sense of loss in her life that he did. His mother was a fine woman who would do any man proud as his wife. Jack prayed every day that she'd find the happiness and security she deserved.

"I'll head out in the morning," he said, pulling out a chair at the long dining table. He rested his cup on the crocheted tablecloth and wondered how long it would be before Grace Reilly was done "resting." "Mind if I stay the night?"

"Your room is ready," his mother said. "Anytime you get the inclination."

She joined him at the table, stirring sugar into her coffee cup, and though she didn't say it, Jack knew how much she missed seeing him more. But his life now involved being a cowboy with the Wells Cattle Company. It wasn't unusual for weeks to go by before he found an opportunity to ride into Great Falls.

Might be Grace Reilly could give him one, now and again.

"You know anything about her?" he asked, taking a sip of hot brew to warm his belly. "Grace, I mean."

"No. Except that she's here to see Allie Gibson."

His brow rose. "Allie?"

"She didn't say why, but I'd guess Allie wasn't expecting her. Otherwise, I'm sure she would have met her at the train."

"She would."

Mick hadn't been expecting her, either. Granted, he'd been out riding with the posse, but Jack was certain Allie would've sent word that a friend of hers was due in.

Jack's curiosity about Grace deepened, but before he

could speculate about her further, a knock sounded on the front door.

"Anyone you know coming to call?" he asked, rising.

"No. No one." His mother shook her head.

"I'll see to it, then."

He opened the door to a swirl of cold air and a man standing on the threshold. Unshaven, barely bundled against the night, he touched the brim of his hat in greeting.

"You got a woman by the name of Grace Reilly staying here?" he asked.

Jack turned wary in a hurry. "Who's asking?"

"Got her trunk here. From the train station. Just delivering it to her, that's all."

Jack's glance dropped to the rectangular shape sitting on the porch. He recalled Grace's black satchel in the restaurant, but she'd had no other baggage with her than that. At least, not that he'd noticed.

He inclined his head and opened the door wider. "Upstairs. Need some help?"

"I got it."

"Room 3," Camille said. She pointed toward the stairs. "At the end of the hall."

"Obliged, ma'am."

The railroad attendant dragged the trunk in, then hefted it onto his shoulder. Without a backward glance, he headed past them toward the sleeping rooms, dragging snow in his wake.

And Jack vowed, as soon as the man left, he was going up to see Grace Reilly, too.

A heavy-handed knock startled Grace from her dozing. Her sluggish mind strove to comprehend where she was, what the noise could be, who would be here demanding that she get up and answer the door—

She sat bolt-upright. Her fingers flew to her hair and tidied errant strands. They smoothed her bodice and checked her buttons as she swept aside her skirts and scrambled off the bed.

It was likely Camille checking on her. Already, the woman felt like a friend, someone to be trusted. Grace didn't know what she would've done without her help, or Margaret's, after the savage attempted to kidnap her. Both women had fretted over her like she was a helpless pup caught in quicksand.

Which she'd been, of course. And sinking fast.

Grace hurried to open the door. Her smile stalled on her lips; she stared in stunned surprise at the man waiting in the hall.

Her half brother, Carl.

He hadn't changed in the time since she'd seen him last. Same lean, wiry body. Same long sideburns and scruffy moustache. Same long brown hair pulled back in a straggly queue. He even wore the same filthy hat she remembered—with its concho-studded hat band and a bent quail feather.

"Carl!" she exclaimed. "How did you—?"

"Quiet!" he snarled, slashing a glance down the hall and toward the stairwell, as if to see if anyone was coming up. Or going down. No one was, and he angled past her with one quick stride, entered the room and closed the door.

Grace's gaze narrowed knowingly. "You're in trouble again, aren't you?"

"What makes you think so?"

"Because you usually are."

"Don't go hopping on your soapbox with me, Grace." He scowled. "It's nothing I can't handle."

His arrogance both baffled and exasperated her. Living an honest life, or working a decent job, had never mattered to him. Instead he chose to skirmish with the law, always forced to stay one step ahead of jail time or a lawman's bullet.

Like their mother. Bess Reilly had a wild streak in her, too, that ended only with her death.

The somber thought swept away Grace's disapproval and dropped a rush of worry into its place. Carl might be shiftless and no-good, but he was her brother, the only kin she had left. He just needed someone to take care of him now and again. Give him the direction he needed, whether he appreciated it or not.

Which most times, he didn't.

"Are you hungry?" she asked. "I can get you something to eat downstairs."

"No," he said sharply.

"Have a seat and warm up, then." Acutely aware he

intended to stay out of sight, at least for the moment, she indicated the fire snapping in the hearth. "It's bitter outside."

"I can't stay," he said.

She regarded him, thinking again how thin he looked. How *worn*. Her heart squeezed. "Is it money again? Is that what you want?"

"I'm here, doing you a favor."

She drew back in wary surprise. Carl Reilly had never done a favor for her or anyone else in his troubled life. "What kind of favor?"

"I brought your trunk from the train station. It's sitting in the hall."

Taken aback, she opened the door, just to make sure he was telling her the truth, and there the trunk sat, on the crimson floral carpet. One glance at the leather straps and distinctive brass latch engraved with her initials confirmed it was hers. In her surprise at seeing him, she hadn't noticed it was there.

"How did you find me here?" she asked, turning suspicious. "How did you claim my luggage, when you never met me at the train?"

"I just asked a few questions at the station and then I figured it out, that's all," he said, talking fast. "I came here 'cuz I got to talk to you. It's real important."

Thinking of Camille downstairs, Grace shut the door again. Firmly. "I'm listening."

"It's about Ma," he said, a cold gleam in his eyes. "I found the last of her killers. The one left standing."

Her heart fell into a slow, thunderous pounding inside her chest. The last killer. The man who'd been responsible for their mother's death. A single shot fired by a member of the posse during an ambush near the Cimarron River, just outside of Folsom, in New Mexico Territory.

Grace would never know who pulled the trigger or whose bullet claimed Bess Reilly's life. No one would. But Grace knew there were six men in Sheriff Edward Farr's posse and that just by being there, lying in wait for the Ketchum brothers' gang, each one was as responsible for her mother's killing as the other.

Grace knew, too, all of them had died in the shoot-out.

Except one.

She lifted trembling fingers to her mouth and teetered on the edge of profundity.

"Who is he?" she whispered.

"Jack Ketchum," he said, triumphant. "But he goes by Hollister now." A feral smile darkened his wind-chapped lips. "And he's right downstairs."

Grace hissed in a breath of shock. Hollister. Camille's son, Jack? The one who had saved her from the stranger's kidnapping attempt?

"Hollister's breathing down my neck, Grace. He's working with the law again."

"Why is he looking for you?" Her alarm grew. Jack had confronted the long-haired stranger this afternoon without a shred of fear. She could only imagine the courage he'd shown, too, that awful day when his posse battled with her mother's gang, defying the gunfire erupting around him. He was a man who wasn't afraid to confront danger; he lived and breathed justice. "What have you done, Carl?"

"I ain't telling you the details. But I'm telling you this. I'll kill him, Grace, if he gets too close. I'm not going to let him do to me what he did to Ma."

Grace's throat closed, holding back the truth hammering inside her conscience. The knowledge, difficult to admit even to herself, that it had been her mother's crimes, nothing else, which landed her in the posse's path. Crimes she'd taken part in of her own volition, her own stubborn disregard for what was right and what was wrong. In her desperation to outwit them, she'd fought the lawmen, and they'd fought back.

It would forever be Grace's biggest loss that there'd been no winners that day. No survivors except Jack Ketchum.

Hollister, she corrected. Jack *Hollister*.

Bess Reilly had suffered the consequences from bad decisions, but Grace couldn't tell Carl as much. He was too much like their mother, too unfettered and callous to listen to reason. To care.

Grace, on the other hand, was bred to her grandmother's thinking. Lucille Reilly had despaired of her only daughter's penchant for crime, but she'd taken Grace in and raised her as her own. Through her, Grace had learned about honesty and virtue, respect for the law and contempt for anything that rode against it.

Out of love and desperation, Grandmother had saved Grace from a life of crime.

Now, whether he appreciated it or not, it was Grace's turn to do the same for Carl.

Chapter Four

The vow had barely settled into Grace's brain before the door swung open. A rude and unexpected intrusion into the privacy of her room that pulled a startled gasp right out of her.

But the man standing in the doorway, one hand gripped on the knob, the other curled around the butt of his Colt, didn't notice.

Suspicion darkened his expression. His sharp glance latched on to Carl, like a wolf over a meaty bone. Clearly alarmed, Carl took a swift step backward.

Jack Hollister. Seeing him now, again, a strange new fascination coiled through Grace, like ribbon around a maypole.

He had the look of a lawman about him that she hadn't noticed earlier in Margaret's Eatery. A calculated way of holding his body, like a predator on the hunt. As if he prepared himself for attack against whatever he encountered.

Power. He had that, too. A cold kind of power that warned he wasn't a man to be crossed. He was a man who could take care of himself and anyone else he chose to protect. God forbid the unlucky soul who dared to defy him.

Like Mama.

She wouldn't have had a chance against him. Had she been afraid? Was there time to regret her sins? What would it have been like to face down a whole *posse* of men like Jack Hollister?

Grace's eyes stung from the pain of her mother's mistakes. Why couldn't she understand the life she led would inevitably end in violence?

And yet…as Grace stood there, riveted in time, a lone detail about that terrible day surfaced from the fringes of her memory. Information she'd gleaned about the last man standing.

Sam Ketchum had died at the hands of his own son.

Jack understood violence.

He'd suffered, too.

"What the hell is going on in here?" he growled. Though it appeared he spoke to both of them, he leveled hard eyes over Carl.

Carl lifted his hands. "Whoa, mister! Ain't nothing wrong going on, all right? Nothing."

Jack swiveled his head toward Grace and raked his gaze over her. "You okay?"

"I'm fine. He brought my trunk," she said in an unsteady voice. "From the train station."

"Yet it sits in the hall. And your door is closed."

"Yes." She conceded how it must look to him. The impropriety of it. And the risks. Did he have an inkling of who Carl really was? "We were chatting, that's all."

"Chatting."

"I was just leaving, too." Carl jerked his chin toward the open door. "And I will, once you put away that shooting iron of yours."

A moment passed, as if Jack warred with his inability to trust. Or believe. Finally he nodded. His stance eased, but the Colt remained leveled. He stepped away from the door, deeper into the room. "You can let yourself out."

"I'll do that."

Carl headed toward the hall, but paused long enough to acknowledge Grace with a nod.

She understood the unspoken message he gave. The warning that he wouldn't always be so agreeable with Jack Hollister, that when their paths crossed again, it wouldn't be pretty.

Swallowing hard, Grace forced a cool smile. "Thank you for bringing my trunk in this frightfully cold weather. I do appreciate it."

"Glad to help, ma'am."

Carl made his escape, and Jack stepped into the hall

to watch him descend the stairs, making sure he left without causing trouble. Striving to calm her scattered nerves, Grace busied herself by striking a match and lighting the lamp. She kept her movements careful, controlled, making it appear as if everything she did was the perfectly normal thing to do.

When she was feeling anything but normal. How did a woman act when she was left alone with the man partially responsible for her mother's death? Or God forbid, if it came to it, her recalcitrant half brother's, too?

Downstairs, the front door slammed. Jack appeared in her doorway again.

"Where do you want your trunk?" he asked.

The low timbre of his voice reached her from across the room. No longer threatening, but deeply masculine and…appealing.

She squelched the thought. It wouldn't do to be so easily affected by him, by something as silly as hearing him talk. She gestured toward a space along the wall. "Over there would be fine."

Hefting the trunk appeared effortless for him, and after setting it where she'd indicated, he straightened, strode toward the door and closed it. He turned toward her, apparently unconcerned by the impropriety of being with her, an unmarried woman, like this.

Grace wondered why he didn't leave. Mostly she wondered if she should be afraid…

For a moment, a strange sense of intimacy encircled

her. The two of them in her small, unassuming sleeping room. Jack Hollister filled the space with his presence, and the lamplight wrapped around him, taking away the shadows and gifting her with her first real glimpse of the man who'd participated in the carnage leading to her mother's death.

Grace gave into the curiosity and allowed herself to stare. He was different now than he'd been with Carl. No longer a predator with the skill and inclination to kill.

Instead just an ordinary cowboy.

This new, unexpected side of him intrigued her. She'd never seen a real cowboy before, but from the toes of his scuffed boots, past his denim-clad thighs, and up to the red bandanna tied loosely around his throat, Jack Hollister epitomized this wild land. Hair the golden color of buckskin hung past the collar of his shirt, the ends just reaching his shoulders and held back from his face with a careless sweep of his fingers.

Yet of anything, it was the scar on his cheek that gave him a ruthless look, a titillating sign of how he'd once lived with danger, and Grace was hard-pressed to keep the forbidden zing of excitement firmly—and properly—out of her blood.

All too aware of how he watched her, too, as if she consumed his every thought, she gathered her wits tightly around her and attempted to break the disconcerting web that had spun itself around them.

"I don't believe we've been properly introduced," she said. "My name is—"

"Grace Reilly. I know."

She cocked her head, not altogether surprised that he already knew. How else would he have found her at Lindell's?

"Camille must have told you about me," Grace said.

"She did."

"She's a lovely lady."

Again Grace recalled the kindnesses the woman had showed her. Where would she be now, tonight, without Camille's help?

"They don't come any finer," he said. He regarded her. "She's my mother."

"Yes. She told me."

Camille and Jack. Mother and son. Grace couldn't see much resemblance between the two. The same gray-green eyes, she supposed. And the same shade of dark golden hair, but there, the similarities ended.

"Then she would've told you my name is Jack Hollister," he said with a smile that could've melted butter.

"She did."

A belated realization that her response was an exact match to his landed an answering smile onto her own lips, but she quickly stifled it. She couldn't let herself relax with this man. He didn't yet know Bess was her mother, or that Carl was her half brother, and if he did, he wouldn't be so quick to give her one of his buttery-smooth smiles.

Nor would he be pleased to learn that Carl would just as soon kill him as see him breathe, and Grace had to do everything she could to protect them both.

The lamplight shrouded her in softness, and if he didn't know better, Jack would have thought she'd floated down from heaven on a cloud.

An angel draped in blue.

Full and thick, the color of rich sable, her hair framed her face in precisely pinned, fashionable rolls. Not a single strand appeared out of place, despite the fact she'd just been resting. Traveling, too, for who knew how many days.

He fisted his hand against a strong craving to feel the silken mass. To experience its weight sliding through his fingers.

"I must thank you for saving me from that horrid man this afternoon, Jack," Grace said quietly. "If you hadn't, the consequences would have been unthinkable."

"So don't," he said huskily.

"Think about it? How can I not?" Her lashes, as rich and thick as her hair, lifted. Perfect crescents framing her blue, blue eyes. "It's not something I can forget."

In the rush of sympathy that swept through him, an intelligent response escaped him. It was likely the truth. Wouldn't be easy for anyone to keep from reliving what she'd gone through.

"Hell of a scare, for sure," he said finally and cocked his jaw from how trite the comment sounded.

For a moment, she said nothing, and those blue eyes clouded before glancing away. He sensed her distress went deeper than she let on, triggering him to wonder what she wasn't telling him.

"Would you like to sit down?" Her composure collected again, she extended her arm, slender like the rest of her, and indicated a plain wooden chair near the fire.

"No, thanks. I'll stand," he said.

But his glance slid toward the bed behind her. Topped with a red-and-brown checkered quilt and wide enough for both of them to sit.

Or lay.

His blood began a slow and steady warming from the thought of what it would be like to fall back onto that quilt with her. Damned if she wasn't one hell of a distraction. Lusting over her wasn't why he was here. And what made him think she'd even *want* to sprawl on the quilt with him? A scar-faced ex-lawman who turned cowboy to escape the ugliness of his past?

He scowled, jerked his glance back and found her watching him. Defiantly. As if she knew exactly why his eyes had strayed behind her.

No shrinking violet, this one. Yet a faint blush touched her cheeks, and Jack knew she wasn't as unaffected by the thought of them on the bed as she'd like him to think.

"You have any idea who he was?" he demanded roughly, changing the subject to one less far-fetched and giving him the advantage, something to sink his teeth into. To keep from thinking of things he shouldn't.

His gruffness startled her. "The stranger from this afternoon, you mean?"

"Why would he want to kidnap you?"

"I have no idea." She crossed her arms and shivered. "I never saw him before, and I hope I never do again."

Jack let the comment pass. Whoever the lowlife was, he'd had a reason for attempting his attack. It wouldn't matter that he'd failed. He'd just try again.

"Do you have a husband?" Jack blurted the question chafing under his skin. "Someone the stranger might use you against?"

"Like a vendetta? For ransom?" She appeared appalled at the idea and shook her head emphatically. "Absolutely not. I'm not married yet, Jack. And if I were, no husband of mine would have dealings with the likes of him."

"Then how would he have known you were here, fresh off the train?"

"I don't know. Believe me, I've wondered that very thing myself. All I know is he was watching me. I'm sure I was simply a—a spontaneous—"

"No," Jack said sharply. "You weren't. The risks were too great for him to just steal you away in broad daylight."

"But the streets and boardwalks were deserted. There was no one around to see."

"He had motive, Grace. Motive."

Her throat worked. Jack knew he was scaring her, but she had to understand how much danger she was in. Every lawman knew crime at any level always started with a reason, however misguided.

"Robbery, perhaps," she said hesitantly. "I dress well, and he would've assumed I was wealthy."

"Yet he never took your purse. Or your leather satchel."

She paled. "No."

"If it was money he wanted, why didn't he just rob the restaurant? The day had been a busy one. The till would've been full."

A shaky breath slipped through her lips. "True."

Jack tried another angle. "Where were you headed when he grabbed you?"

She hesitated. "To the police station."

Jack's brow arched. That he hadn't expected. "Because?"

"I needed help finding a friend, but then I changed my mind, and—"

"Allie Gibson," Jack said, reiterating what his mother had already told him.

"Paris," Grace corrected quickly. "*Paris* Gibson."

Paris? Jack wondered if Camille had been wrong in her information. Or if Jack had somehow misunderstood.

His gut told him neither one. Didn't make sense that

Grace would've traveled so far to see a man old enough to be her father. And in the time Jack had known him, Paris had never mentioned her.

He grunted and once again had the feeling she was hiding something. "You wouldn't have found him in his apartment, Grace. He left for Minnesota a week ago."

"He did?" She sank down onto the side of the bed as if the information had blindsided her. "I had no idea."

She turned silent so long, Jack felt compelled to keep talking.

"He went back there to hire a private investigator for Allie. She's in a heap of trouble, and there's a fair number of us who believe she's innocent. Her father's doing what he can to sort things out."

Her eyes rounded. "You know about Allethaire's troubles?"

"Every detail." Of how a forged draft found its way into a fat envelope of cold, hard cash planted in her traveling trunk. Evidence linking her to an embezzling scheme back in Minneapolis, then robbed minutes afterward by a gang headed up by a man named Boone. Jack nodded grimly. "She told us."

Clearly restless, Grace stood again and strode toward the window. She stared, pensive, through the glass panes into the black night outside.

"She left Minneapolis in such a hurry," she said softly, almost to herself. "The scandal was about to break, and she must've been so frightened over it. Her reputation was on the brink of being ruined. I can only imagine how awful this whole ordeal has been for her." Grace whirled back toward him with her brows furrowed in puzzlement. "You call her 'Allie.' Why? I've always known her as 'Allethaire'."

He shrugged. It had been Mick who insisted on using her nickname since he found her given name far too pretentious. "It's a different life out here for her. Guess she was ready for a change."

"How is she, Jack? Is she holding up all right?"

"She's fine."

He declined to tell her that, in truth, she was more than fine. Probably happier than she'd ever been in her whole life. Mick had asked her to marry him, and she'd agreed, and she was likely planning the details of her spring wedding at this very moment.

But Jack would let Allie tell Grace her news. It was just the sort of thing females liked to talk about.

"How can she be fine?" Grace demanded. "She has to be devastated by all that's happened."

"She's *fine*," he said again. "I promise."

Grace stared at him. Then, she spun toward her blue coat, hanging next to the door. "I'd like to see her. Now. Tonight." She grabbed her hat. "Would you take me there?"

Jack hooked a thumb into his hip pocket. "Take you where?"

"To her father's apartment."

"She's not staying there," he said slowly.

She went still. "But you said she's here. In Great Falls."

Jack pursed his lips. "I never said that."

Bemused, she frowned. "But you said you talked to her."

"I did. She's staying at the WCC—"

"The Wells Cattle Company?"

"One of the biggest spreads around."

Her breath left her in a gush. "So Allethaire has told me."

"Paris is building his hydroelectric plant there, on Wells land."

"Yes. She told me that, too. She's very proud of him for it."

To say the power plant was crucial to the prosperity of the entire territory and one more feather in Paris's prominent hat was an understatement.

"That's where I live," Jack said. "At the WCC."

"As one of their cowboys?" She appeared taken aback.

He didn't move. It wasn't so long ago being a cowboy was just what he wanted to do. Immerse himself in a safe, mindless job. To start over in a new life and forget the failures of his past.

But somehow, with her, it felt so damned…menial. Like he'd never had aspirations for anything more than that.

She wouldn't know how everything he'd ever worked for, dreamed about and succeeded at had been destroyed, thanks to his old man. Nor would she know about out-laws or betrayal, of blood fighting against blood.

Grace Reilly had only known how perfect life could be.

He scowled at their differences. "That's right. I'm one of their cowboys. So I know for a fact it's too far and too late to ride out there tonight."

"I understand." She appeared so disappointed, guilt rolled through Jack for denying her. She peered at him beneath those dark crescent lashes of hers. And his knees went weak. "Could we see Allethaire tomorrow?"

That she wanted him to take her instead of hiring someone else startled Jack. That she only intended to use him as a means of transportation didn't.

What red-blooded man would deny her?

"We'll head out around noon," he said gruffly. "Should be warmer then."

"Yes, of course."

Abruptly aware, then, of how he'd spent the last week on the back of a horse, that he needed a bath, a shave and a set of clean clothes, he turned on his heel to leave.

"Jack?"

He halted in midstep. Turned back around to face her.

She strode toward him, her skirts rustling with every slow, purposeful step. She placed a hand on his arm, her touch as bold as it was seductive. Her full mouth softened.

"Thank you again for all you're doing for me," she said softly.

She turned his brain to mush. Seared his skin with the warmth of her hand, and branded the sweetness of her voice into his memory.

Mostly Grace Reilly filled him with the certainty that having met her, his life—and his heart—would never be the same again.

Chapter Five

The next morning, after Grace dressed, fixed her hair and made the bed, she parted the drapes covering the only window in her room. The day had dawned bright and crisp-cold, with a deep azure sky that stretched nearly cloudless. A heavy blanket of snow had fallen overnight and painted the yard a pristine white. In contrast, the street running along the front of Lindell's Boardinghouse had already been muddied and rutted by trampling horse hooves and wagon wheels.

Her perusal shifted to the tree growing tall past the house's roofline, close to the window. A bird had flown into the tangled canopy of naked branches and perched contentedly, only a few feet away, directly in Grace's view.

The little snippet of crimson was unexpected and striking amidst the tree's winter dreariness, and recognizing the species, Grace clucked her tongue in delighted surprise. Her grandmother had been an avid birdwatcher, a hobby that Grace had learned to enjoy with her, and though she considered herself a mere amateur, Grace knew this little bird was a rarity in the territory for this time of year.

The Redheaded Woodpecker had strayed from its usual migration toward a warmer climate, and the novelty of seeing him this late in the year compelled Grace to rush to her satchel for her camera. With the Kodak in one hand, she wrestled the window open with the other. Brisk cold assailed her, but she didn't bother going for her shawl. She didn't dare lose this opportunity to capture the woodpecker's image on film. What a prize to show her birdwatching club when she returned to Minneapolis!

She leaned out the window as far as she could, and balancing the black box-shaped camera in her left hand, she leveled her gaze downward and centered the bird in the lens. With her right hand, she pulled the cord to cock the shutter, advanced the film with the camera's key, then pressed the trigger, all in three efficient and well-practiced motions.

"Perfect!" she breathed.

As if he sensed Grace got what she wanted and had no further need of him, the woodpecker opened his wings and fluttered away. Grace withdrew and closed the window.

The camera was one of her most prized possessions,

a gift from Grandmother last Christmas. Grace wasn't often without it, for reasons just like this one, the fun and spontaneity the Redheaded Woodpecker presented, and hadn't the little creature been a model subject?

Unlike Charles Renner, who used to resist most every time she wanted to take *his* picture.

She sobered at the sudden thought of her former business partner and the Literary Aid Society's liaison within the Minneapolis community. At first, his help in organizing their endeavor to build the grand library the city needed had been invaluable. But his growing arrogance and underlying greed had soon convinced her grandmother trouble was afoot. Time proved she was right, and Charles's power and access to Society funds ended up being the root of all Allethaire's troubles—and Grace's, too.

Unfortunately Grandmother had died before she could provide evidence of her suspicions of an embezzling scheme, and now it was up to Grace to find the truth and see him convicted.

She alone possessed the information to do that—by way of the meticulous records her grandmother kept as president and founder of the Ladies Literary Aid Society. Now that Grace had taken over in her place, she was convinced the truth lay hidden in those files. She just needed a little help finding it, that's all. She needed Allethaire, who well understood Grace's inadequacies and would be only too eager to help her comb through the ledgers to read every word and decipher every amount noted in the columns.

Grace knelt in front of her satchel and assured herself the papers were all still there, encased and hidden in the red-ribboned hat box she kept inside.

She tucked her camera away, and with her thoughts still heavy on Charles, she untied the red ribbon and withdrew a manila packet. Inside was a picture she'd taken of him with a friend at a political function.

It had once been her favorite. Soon after meeting him, she'd foolishly fallen for his power, charm and good looks. Even now, she had to concede his handsomeness in the photograph. With his tuxedo and starched white shirt against his dark skin, his black eyes and angular features, his trim moustache and his hair expertly oiled, he'd dazzled her with his smile that night while she focused the lens on both men, glasses of brandy clasped in their hands.

Despite the well-groomed and equally handsome appeal of the other man, she'd had eyes only for Charles. He inspired her admiration, having made a name for himself as a community leader and a rising politician.

But her infatuation had been short-lived and withered altogether with the embezzling charges. Now, she felt only contempt and resentment for the man, and more than ever, she couldn't wait to meet with Allethaire and find the evidence they needed to convict him.

She returned the packet to its place in the hat box,

retied the ribbon and rose. Funny how she couldn't think of Allethaire without thinking of Jack Hollister, too.

How strange to know him now, all these months after her mother's death. Even stranger to know she'd be traveling with him out to the WCC in just a few hours. She should abhor the prospect, she thought on a wave of guilt. Sharing a ride with the man who had a hand, even a remote one, in killing Mama should be unthinkable.

But it wasn't.

He'd had nothing but concern for her from the moment she'd first laid eyes on him. Whether pouring coffee or saving her from an outlaw's devious intentions, Jack had been honorable to a fault, concerned for her welfare, capable of keeping her safe, and what woman wouldn't want to be protected by him?

She owed him her gratitude. Indeed, she must worry more of what he'd do when he found out who *she* really was. Daughter of the wild and unruly Bess Reilly, with a list of crimes as long as his arm, who would have gladly shot him dead if she'd had a chance.

Would he despise Grace for it? Would he feel contempt for the allegiance any daughter would feel for her mother, however misguided, even reluctant? Would he see it as wrong?

And then, of course, there was Carl, in trouble again and refusing to atone for his actions. Jack didn't know of Carl's avowal to kill him; he'd only know how much he disdained her half brother for the wrongs he'd committed, and Grace dreaded the confrontation that Carl warned would ensue.

At least, once Jack took her out to the Wells' ranch, he'd be spared Carl's intentions for a while. And Carl would be spared Jack's.

Reassured, at least for now, Grace wrapped her shawl around her shoulders and left her room. She descended the stairs, and fragrant coffee tantalized her senses. The warm aroma of pancakes and bacon, too.

It appeared the other boarders had already eaten and gone about their day. The dining room table was empty, though the careless placement of the chairs showed their use earlier. Recalling Camille's encouragement to help herself to whatever she needed, Grace headed for the kitchen.

Mixing bowls, utensils and a cookbook lay open on the big table, but the room was empty. A pot of coffee sat on the impressive six-burner stove, and finding a clean cup, Grace poured herself some, added sugar and stirred it in.

An enamel pan of soapy water sat in the sink, and she added her spoon to the rest of the breakfast dishes waiting to be washed.

Most likely, Jack Hollister's were among them. A frivolous thought, but a stubborn one. He struck her as being a man who wouldn't let grass grow under his feet. An early riser. A shrewd lawman like him would make the most of each and every day.

She wondered what time he'd awakened. What he'd eaten. Where he'd gone after breakfast…

Grace blamed her musings on the fact his room was next to hers, and every sound that seeped through the walls last night reminded her he was there. Compelling her to imagine what he was doing. How and why. She'd fallen asleep with him heavy on her mind, and the memories of what he'd done to set up her mother's gang warred with the sheer rugged powerful *appeal* of him.

Pensive, Grace sipped from her coffee and meandered to the window. The warm kitchen had fogged the cold glass panes, and she rubbed away the moisture to better see the blurred shape of someone outside.

Now that she could, the sound of his shovel scuffing against the boardwalk became more evident. Though she couldn't see his face, she knew it was Jack from the way he moved, lifting snow and tossing it aside in steady, rhythmic motions, leaving a long row of neatly piled snow in his wake.

Her glance lingered over him. He made the job look easy, but Grace had shoveled snow often enough in her childhood to know it wasn't. She imagined his muscles working beneath his heavy coat, rolling and bunching across his shoulders, back and down his arms, too.

She sighed, long and frustrated. There she went again. Thinking of him in ways she shouldn't.

She had to remember he would never have a place in her life. She couldn't think of him as Jack Hollister,

Camille's son. That he shoveled snow for the convenience of the patrons of Lindell's Boardinghouse shouldn't matter. She had to continually remind herself of what Carl had told her—he was Jack *Ketchum,* and not so long ago, every outlaw with a lick of sense would have feared him and hated him, all at once.

Including Bess Reilly.

Footsteps at the back door shattered her somber thinking, and she turned just as Camille awkwardly maneuvered her way into the kitchen, her arms loaded with firewood stacked to her chin.

Grace rushed over to shut the door behind her.

"Thank you, and good morning," Camille said in a cheerful voice, her eyes bright from the cold. "I see you found the coffee."

"I did, thank you."

Camille strode toward an iron rack in the corner, close to the stove's wood box. The rack's supply of wood fuel had dwindled, and she clearly intended to refill it.

Grace hastened to set her cup on the big table before reaching for the cut wood. "Here, let me help you."

"Have you eaten?" Camille asked, standing while Grace stacked. "I left bacon for you in the warming closet. It won't take but a minute to whip up some pancakes to go with it."

"Thank you, but I'll just have toast, if that's all right, and I'll make it myself."

Grace refused to have Jack's mother cook for her when Grace was perfectly capable of preparing her own meal. Camille worked hard, both here in the board-inghouse and at Margaret's Eatery, and since it didn't appear she had a husband to take care of her, commis-eration welled inside Grace. She knew what it was like to be alone, too. Losing Grandmother, being left to fend for herself, hadn't been easy.

Which only reminded Grace yet again how she had to keep Carl safe. Somehow. He was all the family she had left.

Grace gave into curiosity and peered up at Camille from her bent position. "Are you employed here at the boardinghouse, too?"

"No, no. Margaret's Eatery keeps me plenty busy. But I like to help with the baking when Mrs. Lindell needs time away. Her elderly mother has taken ill, and she's gone to spend the night with her. She'll be back in time for dinner."

"I see. Well, I still think you deserve a day off now and again," Grace said firmly, rising after the last of the wood had been stacked. She smiled. "Which means I insist on making my own toast."

Smiling, too, Camille nodded. "Then I'll let you. The bread is on the sideboard. While you do that, I'll get more wood. I have several days' worth of baking ahead of me. The oven will be fired up all afternoon."

"Let me," Grace said. It was the least she could do after all Camille had done for her. Besides, what else did she have to do until she could ride out with Jack to see Allethaire?

"All right, then. There's an open shed outside, close to the house. We'll need a couple more loads."

Since Camille hadn't bothered to wear a coat, Grace didn't, either, but she pulled her shawl close to her shoulders, bracing herself for the cold after the warmth of the kitchen. Stepping quickly onto a shoveled path—compliments, no doubt, of Jack—she found the stacked wood just as Camille instructed.

Careful to protect the sleeves of her dress as best she could, Grace filled her arms with the first load. By the time she returned from the kitchen for the second, she was a bit out of breath and invigorated from the weather. So intent on filling her arms again, she didn't see the man stepping around from the back of the shed until he was close enough to touch her.

"Hey, why is *he* still here?" Carl demanded.

In her startled surprise, she nearly lost the pile in her arms.

"Good morning, Carl," she retorted, knowing too well who "he" was.

"I mean it. What's Ketchum doing hanging around this place? How come he ain't gone yet?"

She straightened to face him. "His name is Hollister now. You'd do well to call him such."

"He's still a lawman, and he's still breathing down my neck, no matter what he goes by."

"And if you'd follow the law, you'd have no concern with him."

His eyes, as blue as her own, narrowed. "Don't go getting all uppity on me, Grace."

Exasperation tugged at her patience, and she was hard-pressed to keep her voice even. Carl had always been volatile, and she'd learned long ago he needed to be handled with a gentle hand. Besides, it was too cold to stand out here and engage in a useless argument with him.

"I'm not being uppity, Carl. I worry about you, that's all," she said. "Jack will be leaving soon. He's only here to help with a few chores."

"*'Jack'?*" he mimicked, regarding her suspiciously. "You on a first name basis with him already? Like you're getting all *friendly* with him?"

"He's been nothing but kind to me." She refused to tell him that she intended to ride with Jack out to the Wells ranch later this morning. Imparting the information would only lead to more trouble between them. "I've no quarrel with him."

"Yeah, well." Carl hunched his shoulders in an insolent movement. "He's not on *your* tail. You'd hate him as much as I do if he was." His dark expression pulled into a scowl. "I should've done him in last night when I had the chance."

The shoveling had stopped, and the realization tripped Grace's heart into a fast beat. What if Jack happened along this side of the boardinghouse? What if he found Carl talking to her? Or worse, *heard* him?

"Hush, Carl." Grace couldn't keep the horror from

her voice. "You mustn't plot against him. It's wrong, and no good can come from it."

"Would've been a cinch to go into his room when he was sleeping and unaware." Immersed in his fatal fantasy, Carl's eyes gleamed with ferocity. "Just put the gun to his head—" he mimicked the action, using his fingers for a make-believe revolver, placing them at his temple and pulling the trigger "—and bang! He's dead. Just like that, my life gets easier."

"No. Your life would only get more precarious." A violent shiver racked Grace. She hated seeing this side of him, hated hearing the twisted logic that consumed him. "Go away, Carl." Her voice shook from the plea and the cold gripping her body. The blood chilled in her veins. "I don't want you to come here anymore. It's not safe." *For you, for me. But mostly, for Jack.* She whirled and headed toward the door.

"Wait. I've got something for you, Grace."

Against her better judgment, she halted. Why could Carl control her like this? Why did she let him? "What is it?"

"A message." He reached inside his coat and withdrew a folded paper. He held it out to her. "From Boone."

She made no move to take it. Even if she wanted to, which she didn't, her arms were full, and her hands were numb. She was purely frozen, and if she didn't go inside soon, she'd have to be carried in.

But she gave into careful curiosity. "Who's he?"

Carl squinted a glance around him, for the first time

appearing uneasy. "A friend. He and I are holin' up in the hills a spell."

Grace didn't like the sound of "holin' up." And she knew too well the questionable characters of his "friends." "Why? What have you done this time?"

His chapped mouth pursed. "You gonna keep your mouth shut if I tell you?"

She swallowed hard. "Yes."

"We hit up a train awhile back." His voice lowered. Again, his unease showed. "Things are pretty hot for us right now."

"Oh, Carl." She groaned her dismay.

"But Boone needs to talk to you."

"Why?" She wasn't sure if Carl was telling the truth or if this was one more scheme up his sleeve. "I don't know him, and I don't want to. I can't imagine why he'd want to talk to me about anything." She pivoted, the kitchen and its hot stove pulling her like iron to a magnet.

"He already tried once to talk to you. Yesterday. Leastways until Hollister came along," Carl blurted.

"What?" Assaulted by the memory of the stranger in the fringed coat, she sucked in a horrified breath. "*He* was your friend? Boone?"

His head jerked in a quick nod. "He wants to talk to you about Charles."

She'd lost most of the feeling in her lips, but she managed to whisper the name in surprise. "What about him?"

He waggled the paper in front of her.

"It's all right here. You want me to *read* it to you?" His brow arched innocently.

At the cruel taunt, hurt spiked through her. He'd always known how to pour salt in her most vulnerable raw spot, especially when they were young, and he poured now, with relish.

Irrational tears welled up. He was only manipulating her, using her biggest failure as a weapon against her. Maybe he was telling the truth about Charles, and maybe he wasn't, but if the savage named Boone was using Carl to get to her, to kidnap her, she wanted no part of it.

"No," she gritted. "I don't care about your stupid note. Just go away, Carl. Far away. I don't want to see you anymore."

This time, when she swung away from him, she kept heading to the back door. She refused to let him stop her, no matter what he said or did.

"Hey! Gracee!" Carl's footsteps quickly sounded behind her. "I'm supposed to take you to him. Okay? Just read the note. Here." He stuffed the paper into her numb fingers. "Take as long as you want to read it. I'll be waiting for you, all right?"

Somehow, she managed to wrestle the door open without speaking to him, looking at him, or acknowledging anything he'd done. She stumbled into the kitchen, and Camille glanced up from her bowl of bread dough.

"Is something the matter, Grace?" she asked, a slight knit to her brows.

"No, no. Everything's fine." She kept her eyes averted while she forced her fingers to stack wood. It wouldn't do for Camille to see her upset. She'd only want to know why, and Grace couldn't let her know about Carl. Or Boone. Or the vendetta against Jack. She forced calm into her voice. "I'm just c-cold, that's all."

"I noticed you were outside quite a long time. I should've insisted you wear a coat. Stand by the stove and warm up. I'll get you a cup of hot coffee to wrap your hands around."

Grace's hands were already wrapped around the note Carl had given her, and she couldn't let Camille see that, either.

"I'm fine, really." Only herculean effort kept her teeth from chattering and her tears from showing. Why had she let Carl affect her like this? "I think I'll go up to my room and thaw out."

Camille appeared surprised. "But it's warmer here in the kitchen."

"I've forgotten something up there." It had been so long since she'd had to lie, but Camille hadn't given her a choice with her concern and persistence. "Really, I'll be fine in no time."

"But—"

"I said I'd be fine!"

The words shot out much sharper than Grace intended, and at Camille's stricken look, immediate regret hurtled through her. Tears welled up anew. The woman was only being kind. Her concern had been genuine, and she didn't deserve Grace's rudeness.

She spun away. She didn't want to see how badly she'd hurt Camille's feelings, and she rushed out of the kitchen, through the dining room toward the stairs.

The front door opened, and Jack stepped in, bringing the wintry air with him. His shadowed eyes locked with hers, and Grace's escape faltered.

Dark and ominous, Carl's words thundered into her brain.

Just put the gun to his head...and bang! He's dead.

Sick to her stomach, Grace lifted her skirts and raced up the stairs to her room.

Chapter Six

What the hell?

Jack closed the door and stared after her. If he didn't know better, he'd swear Grace was crying about something.

A loud slam upstairs confirmed her upset. He swung a frowning glance toward his mother, hurrying toward the foot of the stairs, flour on her apron and a towel in her hand.

She halted and cast a worried look upward.

"Oh, dear," she said to herself.

"What happened?"

"I don't know." She sighed and turned toward him, watching while he hung up his coat and hat. "She was fine until she went out for the second load of firewood. When she came in, she acted—" she hesitated, as if trying to put her finger on it "—different."

Jack pondered the closed door. "That so?"

"I don't understand. She was out there longer than usual. Longer than she should have, I guess. Something must've happened, but what?"

"No way I'd know."

But he intended to find out. He didn't normally involve himself with teary females, but in the short time she'd been in Great Falls, Grace had had more than her share of trouble.

And there was something in Jack that wanted to smooth the rough spots she was going through. A woman alone, with her only friend miles away at the Wells Cattle Company—who else did she have to look after her but him?

He headed toward the stairs and took them one at a time, his ear peeled for any sound that might come from her room. At her door, he knocked and only managed to catch her muffled response.

He couldn't know what that little bit of noise meant, so he turned the knob and went in. He found her bent over her trunk, rummaging through its contents until she found what she was looking for. A delicate, embroidered handkerchief.

"You okay?" he asked gently.

She started, as if the sound of his voice was the last thing she expected to hear. She straightened, nodding in jerky movements, and since it looked like she was holding a piece of paper in one fist, she fumbled one-handed to shake out the folds of her handkerchief.

"Of course I am," she sniffed.

"That's what I thought," he said dryly, closing the door and moving closer. "Need some help with that?"

"No."

He took the lacy scrap of fabric anyway, opened it up and handed it back to her. She dried her nose and dabbed her eyes and avoided looking at him. She drew in a breath and let it out again.

"You shouldn't be in here," she said, calmer.

He ignored the comment. More concerned with the lone teardrop on her cheek, he took her handkerchief again.

"You missed one," he said in a low voice, then carefully blotted the drop away.

Odd how she wouldn't look at him. Just as odd, she didn't move away, either. Probably because she was preoccupied with something else, which tromped out any protests she would've been inclined to make.

Jack took heart from her melancholy. He used it to his advantage by knuckling her under the chin to get a good look at her.

Finally their gazes met. Her eyes were darker now. A turbulent hue of blue. Whatever troubled her, troubled her deep. Moisture thickened her lashes. The wintry air had turned her nose and cheeks rosy, and a corner of his mouth lifted.

"Your chin is cold," he said and ran his thumb along the soft curve to prove his point.

Her lips curved downward. "The rest of me is, too."

Jack had taken plenty of risks in his life, but few were as precariously sweet as pulling Grace Reilly into his arms. To warm her, he told himself. She was new in town and didn't know much about him, but she had to realize by now she had nothing to fear from him. From the moment they'd first met, he'd had only her best interests in mind.

Jack inhaled the clean scent of her hair. Took note of how the top of her head just reached his jaw, too. He slid his hand down her back and up again, over her knitted shawl, his senses attuned to the coolness of her body against his chest. She kept her arms folded and her back straight, but her soft exhalation revealed she wasn't completely immune to the comfort he provided.

"Sounds like you were out there longer than you needed to be," he said quietly. "Considering you were just bringing in firewood." He kept talking, rubbing her back, delving for clues into what upset her. He had a strong suspicion whatever it was had something to do with that piece of paper she kept clutched and all but hidden in her hand. "Did you lose your way to the back door?"

"No," she said into his shirt. "Of course not."

Jack waited for more, but no further explanation followed. He'd done plenty of interrogations in his lawman days, and any lawman worth his salt would know by her glib response she was hedging on the truth. Buying time until she could figure a way to dig herself out of the corner he'd boxed her into.

"Someone was out there with you. Isn't that right, Grace? And whoever it was, gave you some sort of message."

Grace stiffened and stepped away from him. "It's none of your business, Jack."

He moved quickly to pluck the paper from her grasp and hold it between two fingers, out of her reach. Her eyes widened, and her jaw dropped in surprise, but as if she considered it futile to try, she made no attempt to take the folded note back.

"No one I know would bring a piece of paper out to a woodshed," Jack said. "Hell of a lot easier to have both hands free to haul the wood inside, don't you think?"

Her chin lifted. "I suppose it would, yes."

"So who gave it to you?"

"Does it matter?"

"To me it does."

"The note is mine, not yours."

Impatience sharpened his voice. "I want to know, Grace."

The long-haired stranger who'd attempted to kidnap her still troubled him, and his curiosity about the circumstances surrounding the note refused to be banked. Might be there was a perfectly logical explanation for it, but who would be acquainted with her besides Margaret, his mother and himself? Especially since Jack was pretty damned sure she'd never been to Great Falls until last night.

"Don't forget innocent people are living in this house." Jack went for a different angle to get her to talk. "Including my own mother. I have to make sure the person who sought you out doesn't have intentions to hurt someone around here."

She appeared taken aback. "No. He wouldn't. I'm sure he wouldn't."

"Yeah? Then who is he? And how can you be sure?"

Her throat moved in her indecision, and she glanced toward the window, as if she hoped to find guidance beyond the panes. Finally she returned her gaze to his.

"The man who delivered the message was the same man who delivered my trunk." The information came grudgingly. "But someone else wrote the note."

Jack hadn't factored in the railroad agent as someone who knew Grace. He should have, and a new hornet's nest of questions buzzed in his mind. Like why the note-writer chose to work through the train station agent instead of approaching Grace himself, for one. And why the train station agent contacted her at the woodshed and not at the front door, like any other messenger would, for another.

"The man who wrote the note—what does he want?" he asked.

"I don't know." Her chin kicked a fraction higher. "I haven't read his message yet."

His brow arched. What woman wouldn't have given into curiosity by now?

"I admire your restraint," he drawled with a touch of sarcasm. He extended his arm toward her, the note still tucked between his fingers. Though he had damned little restraint himself, he succumbed to the courtesy of allowing her to read her own message first. "Here you go. Read away."

"I will. When you leave."

Again, impatience spiked through him. "I'm not leaving until I know what the message says, Grace. I need to make sure everything's all right for you and everyone else around here."

She swallowed. Abruptly she swung away from him to move with thoughtful steps along the width of the room, clearly stalling until she figured out how to proceed next.

Jack's gaze hooked on the blood-warming way her hips swayed when she walked. After she halted and pivoted back toward him, his glance lifted to find her watching him. Had she known how much he enjoyed watching those hips of hers move? Seducing him with every calculated step?

Yeah, he decided. Beautiful women like Grace Reilly always did.

"I was told the note concerns a man I was recently associated with," she said quietly. "Like Allethaire, he's under critical scrutiny for his work with the Literary Aid Society."

Jack's interest sharpened. He mentally sifted through the short list of names Allie had given them to help the investigation. "Who is he?"

She regarded him for so long that Jack was on the brink of repeating the question.

"You're trying to help Allethaire prove her innocence, aren't you, Jack?" she asked in her soft voice.

"Yes." He nodded slowly. "Me, Mick and a whole posse of lawmen."

"Then perhaps I can trust you."

It rankled to see her hesitating. She should know by now how cow-eyed she made him whenever he was with her. Should be clear as rain to her, too, that she could rely on him to do just about anything to help her. What else did he have to do to prove it?

"Listen to me, Grace." He worked hard to keep the impatience out of his voice. "Mick is one of the best friends a man could have, and Allie means the world to him. She means a lot to me, too. Someone is going through a hell of a lot of trouble to destroy her, and none of us knows why."

"I'm quite aware of that."

"One thing we do know is she's innocent. We're all doing our damnedest to help her prove it."

"So am I, Jack." Grace appeared offended he might think otherwise. She thumped a finger over her heart. "Allethaire isn't just a best friend to me. She's the sister

I never had. I'll do everything I know how to expose whoever's incriminating her. I can only imagine the nightmare she's going through right now. For her sake, justice must be served."

He nodded in grim satisfaction. There was little in his life that pleased him more than sweet justice against those who deserved it.

But then, no one knew that better than his father, dead in the ground from Jack's own gun. Sam Ketchum had suffered from justice, all right. He'd died, leaving Jack to a different kind of suffering. A whole wagonload of regret and second-guessing the price justice had cost him.

The ugly memory no sooner came back to haunt him than Jack beat it down with a harsh reminder of that was then, and this was now. Sam Ketchum was notoriously guilty of a whole string of crimes. Allie Gibson wasn't. Because of her, the thirst for justice had been resurrected in Jack all over again, leaving his throat parched with determination to see it done.

"Well, then, Miss Reilly," he drawled. "I'm glad we're in agreement on that at least."

"Justice must be done for Charles, too. I fear he's as guilty as Allethaire is innocent."

"Charles?" Jack's brain hooked on the name.

"Why don't you read the note for both of us, Jack? Then we'll know exactly what it says."

He couldn't yet figure what game she played, dropping all pretense of secrecy between them. Trusting him. Allowing him access to the note before her.

But Charles—with a last name of Renner—was a name Allie had on her list of those deeply involved in the Ladies Literary Aid Society library endeavor. A name Paris had pushed to the top as being suspect, due to some troubling business dealings the two had had years earlier in Minneapolis.

"I'll do that," he said.

He unfolded the paper and read aloud the words written in surprisingly precise penmanship.

"I must meet with you immediately about a serious matter concerning Charles. You know the one."

The color drained from her cheeks. "Read it again, please."

For a moment, Jack debated giving her the slip of paper to read herself, but she looked so worried, he just did as she asked. She listened with a rapt expression, as if she committed the words to memory.

"Thank you," she whispered after he finished.

He turned the paper over. "It's not signed."

"No. I don't suppose it would be."

"Then how the hell are you supposed to know who wrote it?" he growled, impatient again. "And how will you know where to meet him?"

Yet the demanding questions were no sooner out of his mouth when it hit Jack. The train station agent. Of course, he'd know the man who gave him orders to contact Grace. He'd likely been given instructions on where to take her, too, for the rendezvous if and when she agreed.

The soft planes of her face showed her preoccupation. Grace pulled the shawl off her shoulders and dropped it carelessly on the foot of the bed. She crossed her arms under her breasts and meandered to the window to stare into the yard below.

"Boone," she said quietly. "The man who wrote the note is named Boone."

Sweet saints in heaven.

Boone?

Like a fighting mule, the word kicked into him.

Jack knew the name, knew it well. So did Mick. And the police chief. And each man in the posse just back from hunting for the outlaw gang who had robbed Allie of a packet jammed full of money, every dime stolen right out of the Ladies Literary Aid Society's bank account.

Jack's gut insisted the news went beyond coincidence to the biggest lead they'd gotten so far. Key evidence Boone and his partner were still around and closer than any of them realized.

And they'd made Grace their accomplice, whether she realized it or not.

Something Jack had to find out for sure.

"You have any idea who he is?" Jack asked in a low voice.

She turned from the window. "Boone?"

"Yes."

Her gaze remained steady, but he sensed she worked at it. "He's an outlaw, from what I understand. The savage who tried to kidnap me yesterday."

"Sweet saints." The revelation rolled through him. "How did you find *that* out?"

"The person who delivered the message told me Boone wanted to talk to me. That's why he did...what he did." Her throat moved. "Do you know him? Boone, I mean."

"Yeah, I know him." Jack decided to lay all the cards on the table. She had to know who she was up against. And what. "He's part of a three-man gang who jumped onto the train bringing Allie to Montana a couple of weeks ago. Their leader was a known criminal named Reggie who was killed soon after, on Christmas Eve, thanks to Allie's determination and Mick's gun." Jack's mouth quirked at the memory. Their courage had been exemplary; their need for justice equally so. "But Boone escaped into the hills where the third member of the gang holed up. Another lowlife named Carl." Jack paused, watching her cheeks pale. "I'm guessing the 'serious matter' Boone mentions in his note has something to do with the stolen loot."

Her sigh revealed distress. "Yes. I'm sure it does."

"Which makes me more convinced than ever that Charles Renner is involved. Any idea how?"

She glanced away. "I'm sure Allethaire has told you all we know about him."

"Tell me your version."

Some of the color returned to her face, as if just thinking of the man moved the blood in her veins. "He was highly involved in our plans for the library project. In fact, I don't know how we could have done as well as we did without him. He's a shrewd businessman and highly regarded in the Minneapolis community."

But not so well regarded by Paris Gibson, whose opinion mattered to Jack and everyone else in the Great Falls community.

"If the man who delivered the note is Carl, then he's guilty of robbery. A felony." Jack's mouth hardened. "With grounds for arrest."

She moved from the window, as if beset by sudden restlessness. She stepped past Jack, gifting him with the scent of her clean skin and the sight of those swaying hips. When she reached the far side of the bed, she spun back toward him.

"Perhaps we shouldn't be so quick to assume this partner of Boone's—Carl—is as guilty as you say he is."

"The hell we can't."

"I think I should talk to him first. Before you do anything."

"Talk to him?" he demanded, taken aback. "Why?"

"For information." Her voice grew stronger, as if her thoughts took root and fueled her determination. "He trusts me well enough. I can glean information for you about Boone."

Jack moseyed over to the window to stand where she'd been just moments before. His glance latched onto the lone figure, seated on a horse in the shadows. The train station agent. Waiting with the collar of his coat pulled up to his ears, his hands plunged into his pockets, his shoulders hunched against the cold.

Carl?

Grace would've seen him, too, Jack knew. She would've been checking up on him, same as he was.

Protecting him.

He turned back toward her. Noted how she wore blue again, an elegant shade of sapphire from her hems clear to her throat. The rich color accented the creaminess of her skin and lent her hair an even deeper shade of sable.

She looked exquisite standing there, watching him. Untouchable when he wanted nothing more than to touch her all over.

Jack gritted his teeth. Her future had nothing to do with a scar-faced ex-lawman who was finding himself more and more smitten with her, with every minute he spent in her company.

He called himself all kinds of a fool for allowing himself to fall under her spell. But he wasn't stupid. And he wasn't blind.

There was something she wasn't telling him.

Something about Carl.

If he was working with Boone and Charles Renner—and Jack had a strong suspicion he was—then Jack would use every trick in his lawman's book to throw them all into the cooler for good.

But for now, he'd stay right where he was and ignore the need to race outside and nab the outlaw. Jack had to find out if Grace was involved with him first. And if she wasn't, well, hell, her idea of using Carl for information to capture Boone was worth considering.

Jack's feet moved from the window toward her, until he stood in front of her. Close. Maybe too close.

He didn't care. Boldly he curled his fingers around her warm, creamy-skinned neck. With the pad of his thumb, he gently tilted her chin back.

"Yeah, we'll work together to capture Boone," he murmured. "But you're not going to meet with him until I say so."

Her brow lifted to a perfect arch. "Oh?"

"You'll play by my rules, or the deal's off."

She stood without moving, allowing him to touch her. Bold and beautiful and a little reckless, too. "And what might those rules be, Jack Hollister?"

An assortment of stipulations marched through his head, none of them appropriate with a woman who his gut insisted was involved with the outlaw's scheme. Somehow.

"We work together," he said. "You don't do anything, say anything or go anywhere for this case without me."

She opened her mouth.

Then closed it again.

"All right." The agreement sounded reluctant. "Within reason, of course."

Reason? Jack wasn't sure he could ever be totally reasonable when it came to Grace Reilly.

The urge to feel her mouth under his proved it. She was off-limits, at least until he was sure of her innocence, but that didn't stop him from wanting her. To taste her, just this one time…

His head lowered. Her breath hitched, her body fell still. Then, amazingly, her dark lashes drifted closed, and against his thumb, still against her chin, she eased toward him ever so slowly….

Triumph rolled through him, and he drew back, ending the kiss before it ever started.

Jack had always been a man who lived by the rules. Most of the time. He knew how to fight, and he knew how to win. Maybe, just maybe, he had a fighting chance to win Grace for himself.

But he had to get rid of Charles Renner and Boone first. Likely Carl, too.

Only then would Jack know if he could trust her.

Chapter Seven

He didn't know how much longer he could go on living like this.

Boone threw down his pencil and plunged his hands into his hair. His teeth gritted against a roar of frustration and pure unadulterated rage.

It was killing him, waiting for the Revolution to begin. He did nothing but spend his days writing letters that never garnered responses. He lived in squalor, hiding out in an abandoned shack while his stomach knotted in hunger. He spent his nights wondering if the next day would bring recognition and charges of treason. He craved comforts and respect, yet he lived no better than an outcast, as if he were the vermin of the earth.

Viciously, bitterly restless, he bolted to his feet with such force his chair crashed backward. He kicked it aside and grabbed a broken piece of mirror off a narrow shelf.

He stared at his reflection. Disgust welled within him at what he'd become.

An American outlaw on the outside, but inside, he was the Canadian activist, Alexandre Thibault. A name he was proud of, for Alexandre meant "defender of mankind."

It was why he was born. To defend and care for his people in Canada.

He couldn't bear to think what his papa would say if he could see him now with his hair long and unkempt; his once carefully trimmed moustache lost in unshaven bristle; dirty fingernails and a stench on his body from too many days without soap and water.

Boone flung the mirror against the far wall. Shards of glass scattered over the packed dirt floor.

Papa wouldn't like it any more than he did. But as a respected buffalo trader and leader of their people in Manitoba, he would understand what his son had to do for the sake of the Revolution.

Yet what of the great Louis David Riel? How had *he* suffered?

Boone's lip curled. His boyhood friend lived a pampered life as Charles Renner. Far away in civilized society, in the fine bustling city of Minneapolis. Every day he wore his fashionable suits and ate tasty meals on cloth-covered tables. He drank fine wines and smoked expensive cigars.

All in the name of the Revolution.

The jealousy which came all too often of late seethed in Boone's blood. It wasn't fair. When they lived as Alexandre and Louis David, they were like brothers. They'd attended the same school, become fine scholars of philosophy, languages and science, of music and poetry. All of it, they did together.

More important, they were both born Métis and proud of the blood they bore—a mix of Indian, French, Scottish and English. They shared a fierce love for their people and an equally fierce hate for the Anglo Protestant settlers who were squeezing them out of their native lands in the north.

Together, they'd planned the Revolution. To save their heritage, they would defy the Canadian government by establishing their own provisional government.

Boone couldn't deny Charles had been the mastermind. He'd possessed the vision to make the Revolution happen, laying its groundwork under the cover of their disguises, to protect them from the shrewd Canadian agents determined to see them hang.

But it was Boone who provided the bravery to finance the cause.

It was Boone who turned outlaw, robbing trains and stagecoaches to funnel the money into secret accounts set up by Charles.

It was Boone who lived with the danger, who'd taken all the risks.

He had suffered the most.

And he'd had enough. The time had come to act on his own. To make decisions in his own right.

Starting with Jack Hollister and Grace Reilly.

Thinking of them eased his fury. The jealousy cooled. His mind cleared, and his heart lifted with renewed zeal.

Jack was trouble he couldn't afford. Boone had been stunned to learn through the underground that Sam Ketchum's son had drifted north to Montana Territory, cleverly changing his name to his mother's when he went to work at the powerful Wells Cattle Company.

Boone understood revenge. He understood, too, how Jack would burn with it to even the score when he found out what Boone had done to set up his father for ambush. Boone had to get rid of him as soon as he could.

And Grace?

She was the reward for his suffering.

The thought of her heated Boone's loins. Until somewhere outside, a horse blew and vanquished his fantasies. Instantly uneasy, he went for his revolver, strapped to his hips. He pressed his back against the wall, out of sight of the shack's tiny window, and stabbed a sharp glance through the opening.

He recognized the horse trudging up the snowy trail. The man sitting in the saddle with his body huddled tight from the cold.

Carl. Alone.

Boone spat an oath and whipped the door open, uncaring of the frigid air that swirled into him.

"Where is she?" he demanded.

Carl pulled up at the cabin's hitching post. "Still at the boardinghouse."

The news sparked new fury in Boone's blood. "Did you talk to her? Give her my missive?"

"'Course I did." Moving with the stealth of an old man, Carl dismounted. Ice crystals covered his unruly moustache. "She didn't give a rat's ass about either one of us."

His mood fouled again. The pompous bitch. "Did you tell her I wrote the missive?"

"Had to."

Boone glared. "I told you not to."

"You think she'd come with me not knowing who I was taking her to see?" His gloved hands worked awkwardly to tie the reins. Boone understood how cold Carl would be, but he made no move to help him. "Besides, she doesn't know you from a hole in the ground."

Boone gritted his teeth. It was likely the truth. She would better recall him as Alexandre Thibault, a political associate of Charles. She'd met Boone only once before, when Charles had introduced them back in Minneapolis. Boone had never forgotten how appealing she'd been that night. A blue-eyed beauty with a flair for photography...

Again, Boone chafed at being forced to hide his true identity, the name he hungered to take again. What woman would want him as he was now? A filthy, unkempt outlaw?

Even so, he couldn't risk his alias being known. Not when he was wanted for robbing the St. Paul, Minneapolis & Manitoba Railway train. There was a price on his head for it. A posse on his tail, too. Both he and Carl had to keep laying low until the heat of their crime cooled.

"I got tired of waiting on her," Carl muttered, heading for the open door. "So I came on home. You got any coffee on?"

Home? He considered this pathetic shack a "home"?

Boone ignored a bite of disgust, followed him inside and latched the door. "Did anyone see you with her? Or hear you two talking?"

"No. I was careful." He picked up the empty coffeepot and shot Boone an accusing glance. "How come you let this go dry, Boone? You knew I'd be half-froze when I got back."

"I was busy." Boone turned back toward his precious papers stacked in neat piles on the tabletop.

A moment passed. "You been working on those stupid letters this whole time?"

"I was."

"When I told you you needed to go out and bag us some game?"

"Yes." He carefully gathered his writings together, sorting them in proper order for mailing.

Suddenly the coffeepot clattered onto the table and landed on its side. A dribble of black brew leaked out from the spout, staining the wood and narrowly missing his papers.

"Damn you, Boone. We ain't got nothing around here to eat. You expecting me to go out and do the hunting for us, too?"

Unaffected by Carl's whining, Boone moved the coffeepot to the table's far corner, out of reach. "I don't care what you do."

"You don't care about nothing but yourself, y'know that?"

"I'm leaving." Boone grabbed his fringed coat from its hook and pushed his arms into the sleeves. "I won't be gone long."

"Yeah?" Carl glowered daggers of hostility. Boone ignored them, too. "Well, bring us back something to eat. Y'hear me? Else we're both gonna starve to death up here."

Boone made no promises.

He didn't expect Carl to understand how some things were more important than others. He'd never confided his true identity to the man. Never once trusted him to know the content of his letters, the true purpose of his work.

No one knew except Louis David. Alias Charles Renner.

Boone pulled his flat-brimmed hat onto his head, tucked the bundle of papers into his saddlebag and headed outside. He set his sights on Great Falls, sprawled at the base of the hill, and thought of the unfinished job Carl had left for him.

The beautiful blue-eyed woman ripe for plucking.

Jack strode into the police station and found the chief officer engrossed in paperwork.

"Looks like I'm interrupting," he said, quick to shut the morning cold out with a firm latch of the door.

George's surprise at seeing him registered on his ruddy face. He pulled his reading glasses from his nose. "Thought you'd be on your way back to the WCC by now."

"Soon." Jack headed to the potbellied stove and held his hands out to the radiating heat. "Just needed to talk to you first. When you get a minute."

"I'll make time for you. What's on your mind?" George leaned back on two chair legs, and the wood creaked from the strain.

"You know how we just spent a week freezing our asses, looking for Boone?" Jack left the stove and strolled toward a straight-backed chair in front of George's desk; he spun it around and straddled the seat.

"Hell, I'm still not thawed out."

"Nothing but a waste of our time." Even now, Jack could hardly believe it himself.

The police chief frowned. "How so?"

"Seems Boone and Carl have been hiding out right here, under our noses."

The chair landed on all four legs with a loud thump. "The hell you say!"

"I'm guessing in the hills, not far outside of town."

George leveled him with a stern glare, the same one that had struck dread in more than one recalcitrant soul. "You'd better start from the beginning, Jack. And don't leave a single detail out."

Jack obliged, telling him everything he knew, from the moment Grace had been accosted outside of Margaret's Eatery to just a few minutes ago, when Jack discovered the man who had delivered the note—Carl—had slipped away from behind Lindell's, leaving only a confusion of prints in the snow as proof he'd been there at all.

"I'll be damned," George breathed after he'd finished. "The 'Charles' in the message must be tied to the stolen library money since Boone and Carl were the two hooligans who took it. The same 'Charles' Paris is convinced is guilty of involvement in the whole embezzling scheme."

"I'd bet my right arm on it."

"If Charles has been in contact with Boone and Carl about the loot, it'd explain how they knew Grace. By her affiliation with the Literary Aid Society." The lawman fell deep into thought, as if he filed all the information Jack had given him into a special police file in his brain.

"But it doesn't explain why Boone would want to lure her away." The outlaw had tried twice now. What would happen when he tried a third time? The possibilities chilled Jack's blood. "Why involve her at all? Not once has Allie given us an indication that Grace is anything but innocent of any part of their scheme."

George's glance sharpened. "So what do you think? Is she?"

"Innocent?" And wasn't that the million-dollar question? He shrugged. "Not sure yet. But I was there when Boone tried to kidnap her. She fought him like a hellcat."

"And yet she seemed to be different with Carl. How long do you figure he waited for her, out behind the boardinghouse?"

The police chief raised an interesting point. Carl had been alone with her in her sleeping room when he delivered her trunk last night, just as he'd been with her earlier, back by the woodshed. Neither time had he attempted to hurt her.

More important, she hadn't been afraid.

Unlike with his accomplice, Boone.

Jack rubbed his jaw. "I can't figure it."

"I have something to show you." George pushed his glasses back into place and shuffled through the papers on his desk. "Paris sent this information from Minneapolis. I think you'll find it most informative." He pulled out a photograph, then peered over his lenses at Jack. "Might be hard for you to see it, though. It's a picture of your pa's gang."

Of all the things the police chief could've shown

him, a picture of the Ketchum gang was the absolute *last* thing Jack would've put on the list.

Dread coiled through him like a rattlesnake, finding every vulnerable spot Jack had buried deep inside. He didn't think about the old man much these days. He considered himself as healed from a father's sins as a son could be.

Seemed he was wrong.

"Sorry, Jack. If you're not up to it, I'll understand."

As far as Jack knew, only three people in the territory knew he carried outlaw blood in his veins. Mick and Trey Wells. And George Huys. When Jack hired on at the Wells Cattle Company, this close to Great Falls, he'd figured it prudent to let the police chief know who he really was, lest the man read something illicit into why Jack had changed his name. Jack relied on his reputation as a former lawman himself to get George to trust him.

It worked. George had taken Jack's explanation into confidence and not once looked back.

But Jack knew the man never pegged him for a coward. Jack didn't like feeling like one, either.

"Let me see it." He reached across the desk and snatched the photograph from the police chief's grasp.

He forced himself to look, and though there were four faces staring back at him, only one felt like it lifted itself right off the paper and grabbed him by the throat.

His skin turned clammy. Damned surreal to see his

father looking back at him, wide-eyed and smiling, very much alive and as cocky as ever.

But he was dead.

Jack had killed him.

"The photograph was Black Jack's," George said quietly. "Found in his effects after his hanging. Looks like the gang found some time to show off their egos at a studio in Fort Worth, according to the stamp on the back."

"Paris sent this?" Jack turned the photograph over, noted the date written in pencil. About eight months before the deadly shoot-out in New Mexico Territory.

"Yes. He's working with a private detective agency. Based on the description his daughter gave of one of the train robbers, they're hoping the photograph will help with the investigation on our end."

Jack flipped it back again. This time, he studied his uncle's image. Irrational grief for what would never be welled up, but he promptly swallowed it. Black Jack had made a lifetime of lousy decisions; each one had hurt his family in some way. There was nothing more Jack could do for him now.

His scrutiny slid to a third member of the gang. Smaller than the rest. Unsmiling and scrawny-looking with his hat low on his forehead, and his clothes disheveled. Jack didn't recognize him.

The fourth man, standing on the end, turned Jack's blood cold.

The man who had accosted Grace in the alley.

Piercing black eyes. Strong, prominent cheekbones. Tall, long-haired and dark-skinned, he was of a different ethnic descent than the rest.

But it was the fringed coat that cemented a memory dredged up from over a year ago—and left Jack stunned to his toes.

"It's him," he breathed.

"Who?"

Jack's pulse pounded in disbelief. He couldn't move, couldn't speak. The past held him in its choking clutches, throwing him back into New Mexico Territory, deep in the Sierra Grande Mountains. The night he'd been taking his turn as watch while the rest of the posse slept.

"Boone," he growled.

"Are you sure?"

The man who sought him out on the mountain, who had used Jack to set up Boone's own gang for ambush.

His lip curled with hate. "I'm sure."

As sure as any lawman could be when he had nothing else to go on but his gut.

Jack might never be able to prove it. He never saw a face or heard a name. The night had been dark, the man too shrewd, too careful, to give Jack a clue to his identity.

But Jack had gleaned enough from the shadows to remember the hair and the coat. Together, they weren't unusual, yet the photograph was all the proof Jack needed to connect Boone with the Ketchum gang.

And his father's death.

I gotta know...who set me up.

The words landed hard in Jack's thoughts.

Find him for me, y'hear? Will you do that...for your ol' man, Jack?

Suddenly restless, he tossed the photograph onto the desk and pushed himself out of the chair.

"Jack? You all right?"

He strode to the window and stared past the gold block letters arranged across the glass. Across the street, the lights shone in Margaret's Eatery, inviting hungry customers to come in and warm their bellies.

Maybe time had eased the pain from all the wrongs Sam Ketchum had done in his life.

Maybe time had cooled Jack's anger, too, and let in the need for forgiveness.

And maybe, just maybe, the time had come for him to start acting like a son.

George's chair creaked. His footsteps scraped the floor. "Jack?"

Jack realized he had to end the terrible chapter of his father's death. With answers that demanded to be found.

"How do you suppose Carl fits in with all this?" he mused roughly.

"Hard to know. My guess is he hooked up with Boone later. After the Ketchum gang was killed."

"My guess, too."

Who had they been working for?

Charles. Charles. Charles.

Jack's brain pounded with certainty.

One more thing Jack knew for sure. He intended to shatter Charles's game of illusion and deceit by exposing every illicit card he played.

And Grace would be the ace up his sleeve.

Chapter Eight

An investigative trip to the train station proved futile. Jack accompanied the police chief there to glean any information they could on Carl and how he'd found a way to deliver Grace's trunk to Lindell's. No one could recall who claimed her baggage. Seemed one minute it was there, the next it wasn't. In fact, they didn't even know there was a problem until George inquired.

"Suppose he'd been watching her?" Afterward, George paused on the station's platform to light a cigarette. "Then just helped himself to the trunk when he saw her heading to the boardinghouse with your mother?"

"Maybe." Jack squinted in the bright sunlight and thought of how easy it would be to keep track of a woman who was new in town. And alone. "He worked fast, regardless."

Which only made Jack more impatient to get back

to her. She'd be an easy mark now that Carl and Boone knew where she was staying. Jack had a strong need to get her out of town and on her way to the Wells Cattle Company where she'd be safe, right along with Allie.

"Where're you headed next?" he asked, moving toward the boardwalk.

George fell into step with him. "The post office. Been expecting to hear from Paris. Want to walk with me?"

"For a spell. I'm on my way back to Lindell's."

"To see Miss Reilly." Half amused, the police chief tossed him a knowing glance.

A couple of blocks down, the boardinghouse made a wintry sight with its roof almost covered in snow. Seeing it brought on a peculiar warming inside Jack, a reaction he could only attribute to Grace waiting for his return.

"She bears watching, that's all," he said.

"She does." George grew serious. "I'm in full agreement on that. Keep a close eye on her until we can figure out what happened to that stolen money."

He didn't have to tell Jack twice. A buckboard clattered over the rough road in front of them, throwing back slush. Once it was past, they dodged mud and clods of broken dirt to get to the next block. George halted in front of the only post office in Great Falls.

"Come in with me, won't you?" George's firm tone sounded more like a command than a request. "Won't take long. If there's something in there from Paris, I want you to know about it."

Jack soaked in the lawman's trust like salve on an aching wound. It felt good to be involved in an investigation again. Damned good. Justice was always sweeter when he had a hand in winning it.

Not that he wanted Grace left alone any longer than necessary. His mother was with her, and maybe another boarder or two. Jack could spare a few more minutes.

"All right," he said.

Just as George was about to open the door, it flew open. A Jesuit priest bolted onto the boardwalk, his black robes swishing around his ankles. Jack knew him as being fairly new in town, having arrived to head up the new Catholic Church, St. Ann's, being built a couple blocks north. The priest shot a glance along the street. Up one side, down the other.

Jack frowned. "Everything okay, Father?"

"I'm looking for someone. A man wearing a fringed jacket and flat-brimmed hat. Black hair down to here." He indicated his shoulder. "He just left, moments ago. Did you see him?"

Jack's interest sharpened. He shot a glance down both sides of the street, too, right along with George. But saw no one of that description.

Boone's description.

"No. I didn't," Jack growled, swallowing a curse.

"Was there a problem with him?" the police chief demanded.

"Not at all." The Jesuit sighed, then turned to head

back inside. "He could have been someone I once knew. Well, it's a shame I missed him."

Jack exchanged a glance with the lawman, and they both followed the priest inside.

"'Could have been'?" Jack asked.

"Yes." The Jesuit's gaze darted between them, but if he was curious about their interest, he didn't question it. "He was leaving just as I came in. In quite a hurry, I might add. He never even looked at me."

"What makes you think you knew him then?" the lawman asked.

"After I posted my letters, I happened to notice several bundles on the counter. I recognized the name on them as someone who once worked for me."

"Who?" Jack and George demanded in unison.

"Alexandre Thibault."

The expression on the police chief's face mirrored Jack's confusion. The name wasn't in Boone's investiga tion file. In fact, they had no information whatsoever on his family or where he'd come from. He'd always been… just Boone.

"Come. I'll show you." The Jesuit headed toward a young postal clerk, busily sorting pieces of mail and inserting them into their appropriate boxes, lined in rows on the wall. "Might we have a look at that bundle of letters that was sitting here when I came in?" As if to jog the clerk's memory, he tapped the counter with his knuckle in indication of where the bundle had sat.

The clerk appeared wary. "What for?"

"It concerns a robbery case we're working on," George said in an authoritative voice.

"Robbery!" the Jesuit exclaimed.

Jack nodded. "Of the St. Paul, Minneapolis & Manitoba Railway train a couple of weeks ago."

And a whole lot more besides.

"Guess it won't hurt then." The clerk delved into a canvas bag and retrieved several small stacks of envelopes. "Second time he's come in, bringing mail just like this. All of it headed to Canada. Other than that, I don't know anything about him. He's not a friendly sort."

Jack noted how the precise penmanship matched that of the note Grace received from Boone. If he was in fact Alexandre Thibault, then Boone would be French, like his name...

And like the voice in the darkness Jack had never forgotten. The voice that had betrayed his father and the rest of the Ketchum gang.

George pulled out a pad of paper and jotted notes. He leveled the Jesuit with an intent gaze. "This man you thought you saw—you say he used to work for you?"

"Yes, in Dakota Territory, near the Canadian border. I used to run the school at St. Joseph's Mission, and Alexandre was one of my teachers. An intelligent man, as I recall. Very passionate in his beliefs. Rumor at the time claimed he'd come to the mission for political haven."

"That so?"

"Yes. Then he moved somewhere east. Minneapolis, I believe, to join a friend there." He frowned at the post office door, as if in his mind's eye he saw the stranger in the fringed coat all over again. "Perhaps I've been mistaken about him. The Alexandre Thibault I knew looked very different."

"Folks change," George said simply. "Sometimes they don't have a choice."

"Especially if they're on the wrong side of the law," Jack added roughly.

And Boone, they knew, was.

The priest grimaced his agreement. "How unfortunate. Well, I hope I've been a help in your investigation, at least. If you'll excuse me, I must be on my way."

After the Jesuit departed, George checked to see if Paris had sent correspondence and was disappointed to learn he hadn't. Outside the post office, George stuffed his notepad back into his pocket.

"Interesting news the good priest gave us, wasn't it? I'll send out a few wires. See what I can find out on this Thibault," he said.

"Keep me informed."

"I will." Touching a finger to his hat, he hurried off in the direction of the police station.

Leaving Jack behind, gripped with frustration that finding answers was taking too long and grim certainty that Boone was too close.

Dangerously close.

Unmindful of snow-slick boardwalks, Jack broke into a sudden sprint toward Lindell's.

* * *

Of all the things that Grace's grandmother had taught her—and there were legions—making Nut Cake was one of Grace's favorites.

She prided herself on knowing the recipe from memory. It had been her grandmother's specialty, requested by all her friends for their parties and picnics and potlucks. Though Grandmother was always happy to oblige, not once had she shared the list of ingredients or her secrets to its success.

Except with Grace.

In one of her vain idiosyncrasies—making Nut Cake better than anyone else she knew—Grandmother had destroyed the recipe shortly before she died. She solicited a solemn promise from Grace that she never share their secret until she had a daughter of her own, thereby protecting the legacy of the Nut Cake for her own flesh and blood.

Bess Reilly excluded, of course, who never cared one whit about baking a cake or anything else.

Grace had made the vow in equal solemnity. Someday, she would labor over putting the words down on paper for posterity's sake, but for now, she had no need to read them for herself or anyone else. The prized recipe was safely tucked away in her memory.

Grace opened the oven door, waved away the heat and pulled out the pan with a towel to protect her hands. The deep golden color assured her of another success.

A careful poke with a clean broom corn confirmed it was baked to perfection.

Making the treat had given Grace something to do while she waited for Jack to return from his errands. Camille had left for a short time, too, to deliver a couple of her fruit pies to Margaret's Eatery. The Nut Cake was one of Allethaire's favorite treats. She'd appreciate Grace's efforts in making it for her.

Grace shut the oven door and set the pan on the table to cool. She inhaled the cake's warm deliciousness and smiled her satisfaction.

Yet an unexpected feeling of loss swept over her. The unsettling absence of her mother in her life.

Bess Reilly would never know how to make a cake as fine as this one. She'd never follow Grandmother's secret admonitions—to use white sugar instead of brown. To use cold eggs so they would beat better. To line the pan with buttered paper and to know that hickory nuts were *far* tastier than walnuts, any day.

Never. Thanks to Jack.

It didn't matter that her mother hadn't possessed a single bit of inclination for domesticity. Spending time in a warm kitchen baking cakes and memorizing recipes was beyond her interests and abilities.

It only mattered that she was gone. And Grace would forever be denied the pleasure of being with her, inside a kitchen or out.

Her mood turned sad. She tried not to think of the mistakes her mother had made. Her lawless ways, her promiscuity with men, her failures as a parent. Bess Reilly had neither the time nor the desire to raise Grace as her only daughter. But, oh, it hurt to think of how she'd kept Carl, who'd been born as wild as the wind.

Through the years, Grace consoled herself knowing Bess's decisions were out of Grace's control. She couldn't turn back time to make Bess a better mother. She couldn't mold her into a respectable, law-abiding woman.

But mostly, she couldn't make her mother love her.

A blurred shape passed by the front room window and distracted her melancholy. Footsteps clomped on the porch, and the door swung open.

Jack strode inside the house. Even with the distance separating them, he loomed tall and strong. His coat added bulk to his shoulders, making him appear even bigger, more commanding.

Merciful saints, the man had presence.

He had ability, too, and why couldn't Carl see that in him? A dangerous kind of power that elevated him to a level that most men would never achieve.

Abruptly she turned away, snatched a cloth from the pan of soapy water in the sink and busied herself scrubbing the top of the table, which was already clean from when she'd scrubbed it ten minutes ago, while the cake was baking. Carl was a fool to think he could outwit Jack Hollister. The man lived for justice and instilled a terrible certainty within Grace that her half brother would only suffer from it in the end.

"Grace," Jack said.

The low timbre of his voice slid along her skin and through her blood. She supposed she would always remember that about him when their time came to an end. His voice. Masculine, rich, and…unavoidably pleasing.

A throaty sound any woman would long to hear in the dark, Grace admitted with great reluctance. Against her ear. *Very* close to her ear, during the most intimate of nights.

Grace swung back toward him and schooled her features to keep from revealing how he affected her. She didn't want to like anything about the man who would very likely destroy the only family she had left.

"You're back, I see," she said stiffly.

He'd taken off his coat and Stetson, but left his gun belt strapped to his hips. He stood in the doorway dividing the kitchen from the dining room. Grace could smell the cold on him.

He swept a quick glance around her. "Guess everything was all right while I was gone."

For the first time, she noticed the faint heaving of his chest. Had he been worried? Had he rushed back to Lindell's on her account?

That he might have done both rattled the resentment in her heart. There'd been no reason…

"Yes," she said. "I've made a cake for us to take out to the ranch. For Allethaire."

His glance touched on the pan. "So that's what I

smelled." A corner of his mouth lifted, showing his appreciation. "She'll like that." His smile ended. "Are you alone?"

"Yes."

"Where's my mother?"

"At the restaurant. She should be back anytime."

He nodded, and she could feel him relax. Odd that she could sense that about him. He hadn't moved.

Grace regarded him. "Did you get everything done you wanted to do?"

"I did. And then some."

"Good." She untied the apron she'd borrowed from Camille and draped it over the back of a chair. Anticipation for the trip out to the Wells Cattle Company stirred in her veins. She couldn't wait to see Allethaire again. "Will you be ready to leave soon?"

"After I warm up a spell." He watched her. "Do you mind?"

She hadn't considered how cold he'd become from being outside a good portion of the morning. He probably thought her quite selfish, she realized on an unexpected wave of regret.

"Of course I don't mind," she said quickly.

She strode toward the stove and tilted the door open. Heat swirled into the air. "Stand over here, and you'll be warm in no time. Can I get you anything? Coffee? Bread and jelly? It's all fresh."

A few lazy strides took him closer to the opened oven. And to her. "No, but thanks."

She reached for a clean cup anyway and told herself she had to stay in his good graces. What good would it do to alienate him when she needed to save Carl?

"I'm going to give you some coffee, and you'll drink every drop," she said. "You must be chilled to the bone."

Grace had no sooner curled her fingers around the coffeepot handle when Jack curled one long arm around her waist. And pulled her against him.

"I'm not chilled at all," he murmured. "Not anymore, at least."

That voice of his again. Husky. Decidedly seductive. And so low, if they weren't alone, no one would be able to hear what he said but her.

His words weren't lost on her. Or their implication. The oven's heat had already soaked into his Levi's, his cotton shirt, and down to his hard thigh pressed into hers.

Grace released her hold on the coffeepot. She allowed him to turn her more fully against him, and before she knew it, he pulled the china cup from her damp, unresisting fingers and set it safely aside.

The cup she'd forgotten she held.

Mere inches separated their bodies, and yet it was all Grace could do to keep from stepping even closer. She blamed it on the heat. That primal need to share *heat*.

He warmed her, all right. Clear to her toes and back up again. Grace had never been a shy mouse when it came to men, but the feel of his arm against the small of her back marched every nerve in her body into startling awareness.

She tilted her head back and met his bold gaze. Jack Hollister wasn't going to reduce her to the ranks of a blushing schoolgirl. Did he think he could? Was that his intent, weakening her secret resolve to defy him for Carl's sake, brazenly holding her against him like this?

She wasn't going to let him weaken her. She already knew he was a powerful man. Ruthless and rugged. A killer, but only in the name of the law that meant so much to him.

It was as if she'd always known those things about him. She just had to resist his seduction, that's all.

The intriguing gray-green hues in his eyes darkened, and she knew his thoughts centered over her, too. Curiosity surfaced about what he might be thinking. Or liking. Which only inspired a certain headiness that he might find her…attractive and desirable.

But Grace didn't want to dwell on why it would matter what Jack thought of her. In the end, it wouldn't matter, and even if it did, she was much too aware of him, this man she should hate for her mother's death.

He'd shaved this morning. She could see the faint beard he'd left behind, slightly darker than the buckskin color of his hair. Strong cheekbones, lean cheeks, the straight lines of his nose—each pressed themselves into her memory and helped form the distinctive and very male features she could never forget.

Yet it was the scar on the side of his face that compelled her gaze to linger. A narrow slash stretching from his cheek and angling sharply over his cheekbone. Pale, devoid of bristle, ominous. And forever a reminder of how he'd once faced danger head-on.

"Go on, Grace," he growled. "Stare all you want. Get it out of your system."

Her gaze shot up to his. Instantly remorseful, she drew back. "I'm sorry. I didn't mean to be rude."

"Why be sorry?" A muscle moved in his jaw. "Everyone else stares. No reason why you shouldn't, too."

His expression had turned hard, his voice guttural, and for the first time, Grace began to sense what that scar had cost him. And what it had left behind. A deep-seated pain that went far beyond the physical.

She understood pain, too, and compassion urged her to reach up and touch him. To show she wasn't repulsed. That she'd seen things far more disturbing. Gently she traced the ugly line from one end to the other with the pad of her fingertip and imagined the violence that had put it there.

He didn't move beneath her touch. He hardly seemed to breathe. Had anyone dared to touch him like this before?

"How did it happen?" she asked softly.

His strong fingers circled her wrist and slowly pulled her hand downward. Pleasantly warm from the oven's heat, his hand held hers against his chest.

"My father tried to kill me," he said.

The words rolled through her. Was that why he'd killed Sam Ketchum? In self-defense?

Grace should've been shocked. Horrified beyond words. But it hadn't been so long ago that she was a little girl, living with her mother. Grace hadn't forgotten the kind of men Bess Reilly associated with. Their cold-blooded mentality and harsh code of ethics.

The kind of man Sam Ketchum was. So cold-blooded he'd kill his own son.

"I'm sorry, Jack." She swallowed against a surge of sadness. "Truly, I am."

At some point, her other hand had joined the first; both rested against the supple cotton of his shirt. Beneath her palm, his heart beat an angry rhythm.

"Lucky for me, he missed," Jack said.

She frowned at his macabre flippancy. "But not by far."

A scant inch. Less than that, probably, and the bullet would have catapulted into his brain. He would've died instantly...

Of its own traitorous accord, her gaze drifted lower, from his scar and all its unpleasant insinuations, and settled onto his mouth.

The firm, sensual shape held her transfixed and turned her heart sideways. Her thinking, too, toward lips not too thin, not too full. His mouth would be hard, but likely masterful. Seductive, drugging. Meant to ply a woman's.

Hers?

She shouldn't want to kiss him, but Grace flirted with the notion. It would be so easy to. Just once. Raise up on tiptoe, tilt her head back and find out what it would be like to kiss a man like Jack Hollister, a man with outlaw blood in his veins.

Like herself.

Her body leaned toward him, against her will, ever so slightly. Her pulse quickened, and she dared to taunt the fantasy, to see it through....

He went still, as if every muscle inside him stiffened in resistance.

"I've got a score to settle, Grace. Just so you know."

His low voice turned her a bit dizzy, and she blinked.

"I'm hoping you'll help me do it," he murmured.

Beneath thick lashes, his gray-green eyes regarded her intently. Had he seen what she was about to do? Had he known how he affected her? Didn't he care?

She scrambled to gather her wits about her. Her dignity, too. She pushed away from him, needing air.

"What?" she said, too breathless. She fought bitter disappointment that he didn't care about her any more than her mother did. "Help you how?"

"Tell me everything you know about Alexandre Thibault."

Chapter Nine

Alexandre Thibault. Alexandre Thibault.

The words hammered inside Grace's head. She stepped away from Jack while her brain tried to pull the name out from the fringes of her memory.

"Do you know him?" Jack asked.

She'd always prided herself on her ability to recall details, names, faces. Grandmother had called it a gift, but this one, this Alexandre Thibault, remained elusive.

"I don't think so."

She kept her tone cool. His rebuff still stung. Hadn't she been attractive enough for him? Feminine? Appealing?

"Are you sure?" He sounded vaguely desperate.

"No. I'm not. What do *you* know about him?"

Jack rubbed his jaw. "He's Boone."

All thoughts of the kiss fantasy vanished. Her eyes widened. "What?"

"I don't have proof. But I'd stake my life on it."

Grace struggled to comprehend. "I already told you I'd never seen Boone before yesterday, when he tried to kidnap me. Why would I know him or Alexandre Thibault?"

"I was hoping you'd tell me that."

She made a sound of impatience. "You're not making sense, Jack."

"I'll start from the beginning." He shut the oven door and reached for the coffeepot. But he didn't pour. "George and I met a Jesuit priest this morning who thought he knew Thibault. But it was Boone who triggered the thought."

"How?"

"The priest saw him, at the post office."

Alarm rippled through Grace. She recalled Carl and the note Boone had written. "Boone was at the post office? This morning?"

"Afraid so." Looking grim, Jack filled the china cup, then reached for a second. "Seems we just missed him. Anyway, the Jesuit claims this Thibault had some political aspirations and lived in Minneapolis for a time." He glanced up from his pouring. "Which is where you come in."

Alexandre Thibault.

The more Grace repeated the name in her head, the more the walls of her memory shifted and cracked.

"Boone is affiliated with Charles, Grace. We know that. Which means Thibault would be, too."

Alexandre Thibault.

Vague and ghostlike, a strain of familiarity crept in….

"According to the Jesuit, Thibault was French, with ties to Canada." Jack continued talking, beating down the stubborn wall. "We saw the mail he's sending up there. Whatever he's involved in, whoever he's contacting, he's doing so under his real name."

Alexandre Thibault.

Suddenly the wall crumbled and crashed. She gasped, and like water rushing through a dam, she remembered.

Jack went still. "What is it?"

"I'll be right back." She lifted her skirts and dashed past him, out of the kitchen and toward the stairs.

The coffeepot clattered back onto the stove. The china cup followed.

"Where are you going?" he called.

She fled up the stairs. Heavier footsteps followed, taking two to her one. She flung open the door to her room and darted to her satchel, going for the hatbox and the manila packet tucked away inside.

Jack fell to a knee beside her. Fingers fumbling, she pulled the photograph out of the envelope. And stared, as if she were seeing it for the first time.

Except it wasn't Charles she stared at, but the man with him.

"Alexandre Thibault," she breathed. "It's him!"

Jack stared, too, with a deepening frown. "Doesn't look much like Boone, does he?"

She leaned closer, and her shoulder inadvertently pressed against Jack's, hard with muscle beneath his shirt. "Look at his eyes. See how wide-set they are? Boone's were that way." Except she remembered how fierce they'd looked in the alley's shadows. A devil's eyes, not gleaming and bright as depicted in the picture. "And his cheekbones. High and angular. Just like Boone's." She shook her head. "I can't believe it's him!"

Jack grunted. "It's circumstantial evidence at best."

"The similarities are there, though, aren't they? Suggesting they're the same man?"

"Yes, but they're only similarities. Granted, he's got some Indian in him, likely some French, too. Trouble is, the characteristics are shared by a whole bunch of people." Despite Grace's growing convictions, Jack appeared more cautious. The lawman in him, slow to make judgments without facts. "A man can change his hair. He can add a beard or shave one off. But there's one thing he can't change."

Intrigued, Grace met his glance. "What is it?"

"His smile."

Disappointed, Grace frowned. "I never saw Boone smile."

"Neither did I." Jack pointed to the photograph. "But look, Grace. See that left eyetooth? It's a little longer than the right one. And it's crooked. Remember the angle of it, then you'll know for sure if Boone and Thibault are one and the same."

His logic was sound, intelligent, and she took his advice to heart. She wouldn't forget to look at Boone's teeth the next time she saw him.

And she would, she knew. It wouldn't be long before he came looking for her again.

"This is Renner with him, isn't it?" Jack asked, his voice quieter.

Her gaze slid across the photograph, from Alexandre to Charles. Her thoughts sobered.

"Yes." Grace heaved a vexed sigh from the trouble the man had caused. "It's Charles."

"Where did you get this?" Jack indicated the photograph.

"I took the picture, shortly after I met him. Allethaire threw a party for the Ladies Literary Aid Society and introduced us. She was acquainted with him because he'd been a business associate of her father's."

"Did she know Thibault?"

"No, I don't think so. At least, she'd never mentioned him before or since. But then, there were so many of Charles's friends there that night, both within the community and his political circle. It was difficult to remember who was who."

Not that it would've mattered. She'd been soundly smitten by Charles and quite excited to know he'd be working with her and Allethaire on their prized library endeavor. But then, in time, when she'd learned the kind of man he truly was, capable of embezzlement and destroying their hard-won plans for a new library, her infatuation had died, and her need to make him atone for his crimes took over.

"You're a fine photographer, Grace. I've seen few more professional than this." Jack flipped the picture over.

She shrugged. "I dabble in it."

Engrossed with reading the penciled notations she'd made, he didn't respond. Grace peered closer to read the words, too. It had been so long since she'd written them. She narrowed her eyes in concentration.

29 SEP 1885
ALIXNDR THIBO AND CHRLS RENR

Grace's cheeks flamed in growing mortification, and she snatched the photograph away from Jack. She abhorred spelling words as much as she abhorred reading them. She was inept at both, and now Jack would see just how stupid she could be.

But, as she'd long ago learned to do, she buried her humiliation behind the smile she planted on her lips.

"My goodness, what was I thinking? I must've been in a terrible rush when I wrote that." She forced a laugh, the one she'd practiced many times over, and busied herself stuffing the photograph unceremoniously back into the manila packet. "Who knows why I was so careless?"

Jack furrowed a brow. "Thibault is a hard name to spell. You wrote it like it sounds. Doesn't matter."

To me it does. It matters more than anything.

But then, she didn't expect Jack to understand. No one did except Allethaire and Grandmother. Although Carl knew, he only used her humiliating secret against her.

"Main thing is it's proof that Renner was affiliated with Thibault," Jack said.

"I suppose."

Grace didn't care anymore. Her head hurt, and her heart hurt, and she wished Grandmother was here. Allethaire, too. The two people in the world who knew the truth and loved her anyway, in spite of it.

Jack wondered if it was something he said.

He could see the play of emotions on her face. She was fighting tears, and what was that about?

His gaze latched onto her while she shuffled things about in her satchel, more to keep from looking at him than anything else.

"Grace." He gently grasped her chin and turned her toward him. "Everything okay?"

Beneath the crescent of her lashes, her gaze lifted to his. Those eyes of hers—an incredible shade of blue. He'd never seen anything to compare.

But that blue was darker now. Troubled. Confirming his suspicions she was upset about something.

"It's all quite overwhelming, isn't it?" she said.

Her lips curved, as if to make light of her response, but the effort seemed to cost her. A sheen of moisture welled in her eyes.

Jack released her chin. He recalled how everything was fine until he flipped over her photograph and read what she'd written. He had to concede her handwriting was messier than most. Sure, she misspelled the words. Might be she was just embarrassed since females tended to take a little more time with such things. But hell, his own handwriting took some deciphering most days. Who was he to judge?

It was a little thing, besides, and her upset had to go deeper than that.

"If they're guilty of breaking the law, there'll be serious consequences for it," Jack said, mincing no words.

"Charles and Alexandre?"

"Carl, too. All three of them."

Grace sat back on her heels. She cocked her dark head, as if in her mind, she tried to string the jagged pieces of the puzzle together into one neat and tidy line.

"I can certainly understand how Boone and Charles came to be involved in this scheme, but I'm quite baffled how Carl could be so devious."

Jack's eyes narrowed. Carl? He hadn't expected her to defend *him*.

"My impression is that he's simply a pawn in their plan," she added.

"A pawn." Jack scowled. "And yet he was on that train, robbing Allie of her money, quite willingly, I might add, and just as guilty as the rest of his gang."

She nibbled her lip. "There's a sensible explanation for it. We just need to find it."

"Try greed for an explanation," he snapped back. "And plenty of deceit. With some political subterfuge thrown in for good measure."

He didn't even mention betrayal—of her, Allie, the entire Ladies Literary Aid Society, and who knew what else besides?

Damn, the whole thing had turned complicated. What kind of conspiracy was the gang involved in? Something in Canada? And why would Grace have a shred of sympathy for Carl? Who the hell was he and how did he fit into the scheme?

Her mouth curved into a pout. "Don't be angry with me, Jack."

He shifted, resting an arm on one knee to face her. "Not angry. Just itching to shake some sense into you. You've got blinders on, Grace. That worries me. Worries me a lot."

"Blinders?" She appeared surprised at that and laughed; a softly amused sound that curled through the cavern of his chest. "I think you're exaggerating, but I'm touched by your concern."

Behind her, sunlight beamed in through the room's only window and shot sparkles through her hair. Like tiny diamonds tossed over sable satin. Sheer willpower kept Jack from satisfying another itch—to pluck out every hairpin on her beautiful head and watch that glorious mane fall….

Yet the light made her seem small, too. Vulnerable. Somehow. Maybe it was her position on the floor, perched back on her heels. Or maybe it was because she'd traveled so far by herself and ended up alone in Great Falls.

"You need someone to watch over you," he said roughly. "I'm making sure it's going to be me."

Her amusement faded. The sheen returned to her eyes.

The avowal had touched some inner part of her that needed touching, he suspected. Which made him want to touch her, all right. Hold her hard, in his arms.

He gave in to the need. Gripped her shoulders and leaned her back, so far back she had nowhere else to go but on the floor beneath him. He straddled her, ignoring the alarm that flared in her expression, and held her with his gaze.

"You've done a fine job of taking care of me, Jack." She spoke in a voice hardly above a whisper. "That means the world to me. No matter what happens. I want you to know that."

Her hand lifted, and the feel of her palm against his cheek distracted him from an appropriate response. The cheek that bore the scar he despised.

No one had touched him like this before. Without revulsion. Without staring. Without averting their eyes, pretending his disfigurement wasn't there.

No one. Not even his mother, at her most compassionate.

It was as if Grace was oblivious to the ugliness. Like she didn't even know it was there.

But she did, and still it didn't matter.

It didn't matter….

A slow heat slid through his blood, a steady and growing lust for a woman who laid beneath him, as close as a lover, her body pliable and unresisting, while the awareness between them built higher. And higher still.

She'd wanted to kiss him. Earlier, in the kitchen. Jack had sensed it, but he'd resisted it. Any red-blooded man would've taken what she was ready to give, but Jack had held on tight to honor. He was a stranger to her, a woman new in town, with only Allie and a robbery crime to bind them together.

Well, Grace wanted him now.

Again.

It was there, in the quickening of her breathing. The faint heaving of her breasts. The way her hand had slipped over his shoulder and around his neck, tugging him downward…

He took her mouth with a fierceness that left no room for questions, no need for answers. He didn't think of justice. Or revenge. He didn't think of Renner or Boone or Carl, of what was wrong or what was right.

He thought only of Grace. How her mouth moved beneath his with an unrestrained need Jack never expected but couldn't refuse. Grace was passionate, purely female, more perfect than he ever dreamed a woman could be.

He angled his mouth and kissed her harder, deeper. A tiny sigh of primal yearning emerged from her throat, and her lips parted. His tongue delved inward to curl with hers in a seductive dance that set him on fire.

Blazing sweet fire.

She stoked in him a need to have her, all of her, right here on the floral-carpeted floor. He ran a hand over the front of her dress, searching for buttons, ribbons, anything he could tear open to expose the ivory globes of flesh he ached to suckle….

Until the ominous sound of a rifle cocking stopped him cold.

He swore. And spun off her.

Boone loomed in the doorway, a madman with his long tangled hair and fringed coat, and a gun aimed right at them.

Chapter Ten

Grace yelped in horror and scrambled to sit up.

"You're no better than your mother, are you, Grace?" Boone taunted coldly. Feet spread, weapon pointed, he leveled her with a scathing stare. "A whore, just like she was."

"Shut up," Jack snapped.

If he was perplexed about why Boone would say such a thing, he didn't show it. His fingers banded Grace's wrist, and his body shielded hers as he slowly, carefully, stood up. She rose with him, her heart in her throat.

The insult about her mother burned and came perilously close to revealing why Boone knew Bess Reilly, but Grace had to think more of how precarious their situation had become. Jack intended to protect her, but he'd be powerless against a bullet.

Boone's piercing black eyes latched onto Jack. The

rifle jerked. "Take off the gunbelt. Throw it under the bed."

"I want Grace out of here." Jack made no move to obey the command. "She's innocent of everything you're involved in."

"She's *dead* if you don't do what I tell you."

"What do you want?" Still holding onto her, Jack unbuckled the holster with his free hand, each movement methodical. On edge. "You already have the library money, don't you? Thousands of dollars in cash. What else could you want?"

He dropped the gunbelt to the floor. With the toe of his boot, he kicked it into the dark shadows of the bed frame. Grace swallowed at the loss of his only defense.

"I want Grace," Boone said softly. "Hand her over to me."

Jack's fingers tightened over her wrist. "Go to hell."

Boone lifted the rifle higher, to his shoulder, and leveled the barrel over Jack's heart. "Do what I tell you, or you'll die right here."

Only a fool would refuse to believe every chilling word he said. It took every ounce of Grace's dignity and pride to hide her fear and do what she could to prevent him from taking her. She was Bess Reilly's daughter, and Boone had to know she could be as fearless as her mother had once been.

Grace angled her body in front of Jack's, as far as

he'd let her go. Boone studied her with those fierce black eyes, like he could eat her alive.

"You've changed, haven't you, Alexandre?" she said, infusing calm into her voice. "A great deal, in fact."

He jerked. "I don't know what you're talking about."

"You had me fooled at first. I almost didn't recognize you." She shook her head, feigning amazement. "Alexandre Thibault, isn't it? Your real name?"

He went still. Very still.

"Perhaps you don't remember." Grace kept talking to keep her courage up, his defenses down. "We met some time ago. In Minneapolis. My friend, Allethaire—"

"You're wrong."

"—threw a party. You were there, as Charles Renner's guest."

His lip curled, showing a row of strong teeth. And one crooked eyetooth. "You're talking stupidity, woman. Stop it."

"You were quite handsome in your tuxedo, as I recall. You drank brandy that night and had all the ladies in a twitter over you."

Above the collar of his fringed coat, his throat moved. "No."

"Yes. I took your picture. It's become one of my favorites."

A growl erupted from him, like a lion ready to lunge. "Enough, I said!"

"What happened, Alexandre?" Grace knew she

was playing with fire, that it was only a matter of time before she got burned, but still she taunted him. Still, she played with the fire. "Why do you look like—I'm sorry, forgive me—a savage?"

He snarled and grabbed for her.

Jack swore and yanked her back. "Easy, Grace," he hissed under his breath. "Easy."

He kept her pressed to his side, but she ignored his warning. She'd come too far to back down now.

"Was it Charles, Alexandre? Did he force you to live like this?" she asked.

"No one forces me."

Her brow arched at the admission. "You *choose* to live no better than a mongrel dog? Always on the run, with no place of your own?"

"I don't expect you to understand."

"But I want to, Alexandre."

She noted the rifle had lowered. Some. She had his full attention, and was it pain she glimpsed in the steely-black depths? A deep and terrible agony?

"You miss your old life, don't you?" She focused on the pain and tried to make him bleed. "How can you not? The price you pay—for whatever reason you choose—is too much. Don't you agree?"

His breathing had changed. "Some days, yes."

She clucked her tongue in sympathy. "What a shame. You're too handsome and too smart to live an outlaw's life."

"It must be done."

"Because Charles expects it of you? While he's safe and comfortable in Minneapolis?"

Boone's nostrils flared, ever so slightly. The resentment, she sensed, he could barely contain.

"Give yourself up, Boone." Jack spoke roughly. "Cooperate with the law, and maybe the judge will show you some mercy."

The black eyes snapped toward him. "Shut up."

"Show us where the stolen money is."

Boone jerked back to Grace. The rifle's aim turned lethal again. "Come here."

"The hell she will," Jack said, pulling her against him.

Boone jerked toward him. "I'll kill you."

"And hang for it, damn you, with the rest of your crimes."

The air seethed with hostility between the two men, and Grace knew the progress she'd made had been lost. She wanted the library money back as much as Jack did. More. She had to keep trying to beat down Boone's vulnerabilities.

"Alexandre. Listen to me," she pleaded. "If you know where the money is, take us to it. Jack's right. Your cooperation will go a long way—"

"No!"

"That money doesn't belong to you! It belongs to the Society, the people who worked hard to raise it in Minneapolis!"

"It belongs to *my* people!" he thundered. "Who have

none of the extravagances you have and take for granted in this country."

The implication of the words reverberated inside Grace's head and left her speechless. A moment of tense silence followed, until a buzzer sounded.

The door's buzzer.

Someone had come to call. Someone besides one of Lindell's boarders who would've just come inside of their own accord. Boone's head whipped toward the sound; his gaze sliced down the stairs and toward the front door.

Jack took advantage of the distraction and went for the ceramic pitcher on Grace's bureau. He threw it one armed at Boone and yanked Grace to the floor on the far side of the bed where she'd be protected most, then covered her with his body, all in one mind-blurring motion.

Boone twisted back toward them a split second before the vessel slammed into the side of his head, splaying water and knocking his flat-brimmed hat askew. He staggered backward. The skin on his temple split open; blood spurted. His rifle went off, and the sharp report exploded in Grace's ears.

Boone roared in fury. For a moment, rendered immobile from the weight of Jack's body, Grace didn't move, didn't breathe, but felt thankfully aware she'd been spared from the bullet gone wild.

"You all right?" Jack rasped into the top of her head.

Footsteps clomped into the hallway, down the stairs.

"Yes," she gasped, pushing against him. "But oh, we can't let him get away!"

Jack swore and heaved himself off of her. Grace thought of nothing but Boone making his escape, that they had to capture him and get her precious Literary Aid Society money back before they lost it forever.

Tugging aside her skirts, she scrambled to her feet after Jack, who was already bolting into the hall. She ran from the room, too, and had almost reached the top of the stairs when he halted halfway down them. Swore viciously. And raced back up again.

Grace had no time to stop her own momentum, and he clipped her as he ran past, knocking her onto the floor again. She cried out, her legs all akimbo.

"You all right, Grace?" he called for the second time in as many minutes, but he'd already disappeared inside her room, only to run out again moments later with his holster in his hand.

"Yes, just catch him, Jack! Please hurry!"

Downstairs, the kitchen door slammed. Jack dashed past her, slapping the gunbelt around his hips and buckling it while he leaped down the stairs.

"Stay put," he ordered her over his shoulder. "Lock all the doors!"

The front one flung open. A man Grace had never seen before ran in, as tall and lean as Jack. About the same age, too, but darker skinned with jet-black hair.

"What the hell?" Seeing Jack in such a hurry, he froze in midstep. "I heard a shot."

"It was Boone!" Jack snapped.

The man appeared stunned. "Here?"

"Yes, damn it! He ran out the back door."

Jack sprinted into the kitchen, and the other man followed. In the breadth of a heartbeat, the back door clattered shut behind them.

Grace's feet barely touched the carpet on her way down the stairs to see the woman they'd left behind.

Allethaire, as striking as ever in her fashionable chinchilla-trimmed coat and hat, and looking perplexed from all that was happening.

Seeing her flooded Grace with a mix of happiness and relief, and of dismay and horror from her ordeal.

"Oh, Allethaire!" she cried.

Allethaire's arms opened, and Grace fell into them with a shudder.

"I can't believe you're here," Grace said, hugging her friend close and absorbing the cold she brought in with her.

"I nearly had heart failure when I heard that shot ring out," Allethaire said. "Are you all right?"

"I'm fine." Grace pulled back shakily. "Well, half fine."

"Did Jack say it was *Boone* that fired the shot?" Incredulous, Allethaire took each of Grace's hands tightly into her own.

"Yes. Can you believe it?"

"The same Boone that robbed the Manitoba?" Allethaire persisted. "The Boone who robbed me of the Society's money?"

"Yes. He—he just came in here, as free as you please. Of course, all the boarders were gone, and no one was around to stop him. He came up to my room, and Jack was there, and—"

Allethaire's eyes widened. "Jack was in your room?"

On the floor with me, kissing me senseless, making me forget all that he'd done and what he could still do....

But of course, Grace couldn't admit as much to Allethaire. Yet the memory of his mouth rolling over hers, the addictive taste of him, his rugged male scent filling her senses, would remain forever in her mind, so vivid now her pulse tripped, and her blood warmed, and she had the most regrettable urge to do it all over again.

Allethaire's mouth softened. "Well, never mind. He's a fine man. I'm half-crazy about him myself."

"You are?"

"We all think the world of him."

But you don't know what he's done. He helped to kill my mother! And he'll kill Carl, too!

Grace wanted to protest, and again the words didn't come. Allethaire wouldn't understand why Grace had to protect her lawless half brother from Jack. She didn't know the secret Grace had always kept to herself about who Bess and Carl really were. And wouldn't Allethaire take Jack's side of it anyway? Wouldn't she just think that as a former lawman, Jack had to uphold the law, no matter what? That because he took part in the robbery of the Society's money, Carl was guilty and needed to be punished?

Grace let go of Allethaire's hands and crossed her arms over her chest. Her friend wouldn't know that Carl was the only family Grace had left. She wouldn't care that Carl needed to be saved from his crimes.

Pensive, Grace swiveled a glance toward the kitchen door and traded her tumultuous thoughts for those more immediate. She wondered what was happening outside. If Boone was long gone. Or if Jack and his friend had managed to catch up with him….

"Do you think we should go out there and see if they need our help?" she asked, half to herself.

"I think we need to stay right where we are," Allethaire said firmly. "Mick and Jack are far better at this sort of thing than we could ever be. Boone is an awful man and capable of great violence."

"I'm quite aware." In tardy comprehension of what Allethaire had just said, Grace swiveled back to her. "Mick?"

Allethaire removed her glove, finger by finger, and avoided looking at her friend. "You're not going to believe this, I'm afraid, but he's Mikolas Vasco."

The name tumbled out of Grace's memory as the man who had helped kidnap Allethaire in a scandalous ransom scheme three years ago.

"What?" Grace couldn't help a gasp of shock. "The Basque shepherder you told me about who—?"

"The one and the same." Allethaire gripped her glove in her hand and lifted her chin. "I've fallen in love with him, Grace."

Grace blinked.

"We're going to be married, in the spring," Allethaire added.

Grace's fingers flew to her mouth. "Oh!"

"Mick is a wonderful man, truly he is." Allethaire spoke in a rush. "He's strong and honorable and proud. He's half owner of the Wells Cattle Company, you know, which is how he got to be such good friends with Jack."

Grace struggled to comprehend how Allethaire's choice of men had dramatically shifted. A man like Mikolas Vasco couldn't be more different than all her most eligible suitors in Minneapolis combined.

"How could you fall in love with him, Allethaire?" Grace tried not to sound accusing, but unfortunately, she did. "After all he's done?"

"He *saved* me during the train robbery. I practically owe him my life from it. I've never met a man quite like him. He just swept me off my feet with his kindness and goodness, and we've both put the past behind us."

"But, Allethaire."

"Don't you believe two people can change, Grace? I'm a better person for having known him."

Change? Is that what it was? Or was Allethaire

destined to have a life filled with heartache once the veil of infatuation lifted and reality set in?

Grace couldn't help thinking her best friend was making the biggest mistake of her life…and yet she looked so happy now, it was hard for Grace to truly believe it.

Besides, who was she to judge?

Wasn't she doing the same thing as Allethaire? Hadn't she allowed herself to become much too attracted to Jack, his passion and his kisses, so that sometimes she forgot how easily Carl could fall victim to his sense of justice, just like her mother had?

"Grace," Allethaire said gently. Compassion filled her features, and she took Grace's hands into hers again, squeezing them in reassurance. "I learned the hard way I had to trust what was in my heart. I know you will, too."

The back door opened again, and Grace whirled toward the sound. Jack rushed in, his mouth set in a tight, frustrated line.

"How in *hell* many more times is he going to get away from me?" He spat the words, giving fair warning to his foul mood.

"He had the advantage, Jack." Mick strode in after him and closed the door. "We didn't even have a saddled horse ready. And he had a head start on us."

"I'm going after him. I'm not coming back until I have him by the throat." Looking as fierce as he was determined, Jack headed for his coat, hanging on its hook near the front door.

Thinking again how much Carl needed her, would always need her, and now, more than ever, Grace stepped in front of Jack, stopping him.

"Not so fast, Jack," she said coolly. She planted her hand on the broad planes of his chest. The cold which had settled into the fabric of his shirt registered on her palm. "I have a plan, and you're not going anywhere until I tell you what it is."

Chapter Eleven

She calmed him.

Jack had only to gaze down into Grace's upturned face, soak in the beauty that was so much a part of her and the fury up and left him.

Most of it, anyway.

He took the time he needed to clear his mind of Boone, shift gears and let his thoughts take her in instead. His gaze drifted over the perfect bones of her face, her smooth skin the perfect shade of cream and those full, perfectly rosy lips.

They still bore his mark. Slightly swollen and gently parted. Might be his passion had sparked out of control, but she'd matched him, fire for fire.

He would've taken her, right there on the floor, and it took a major intrusion like Boone to keep him from what could've been a big mistake.

Grace would've regretted it. She'd know how Jack wasn't good enough for her. She'd remember how she was bred for the city, to live in high society, mingling with the rich. Minneapolis' finest.

She *wasn't* bred for a cowboy who worked cattle on the Montana frontier. She'd have no admiration for a man who gave up his dream because of his father's sins. A man who succumbed to the shame of being an outlaw's son.

"Before you say anything, Grace, I believe introductions are in order." Allie's voice snapped Jack's thoughts back to the present. She hooked her arm through Mick's and hugged him against her. "I want you to meet the man who will soon be my husband."

Grace withdrew her hand from against Jack's chest and turned. He sensed the apprehension in her. Obviously Allie had told her about the pair's relationship. Jack couldn't blame Grace for being wary, considering the pain Mick had once put Allie through.

Jack curled his fingers around the back of her neck, above the collar of her dress. The warmth of her smooth skin met the cold of his.

"He went through a rough time awhile back, but he's a better man for it," Jack said quietly. "I've never known a finer friend."

Her quick glance showed she appreciated his attempt to assure her. Removing his Stetson, Mick stepped forward, took her hand and gallantly pressed a kiss to her knuckle.

"Mikolas Vasco," he said. "But everyone calls me Mick."

"I must say I'm surprised to meet you, but very happy to do so. You were at the restaurant yesterday, weren't you? With Jack and another gentleman?"

"The police chief, George Huys, yes."

A gracious smile scooted across her lips. "Well, any friend of Allethaire's is a friend of mine. And since Jack likes you so much, then I will, too."

Mick didn't return the smile, but inclined his head in all seriousness. "You don't know how much that means to me."

"You may as well call me 'Allie,' Grace," Allie said. "It's a name that seems to have stuck for me out here."

"Oh?" Grace appeared surprised at that. "How strange to go by something different than what you've always been." She slid Jack a glance through her lashes, turning him wary. "Isn't it, Jack?"

His eye narrowed. There was an insinuation there, in that comment of hers, and he wasn't quite sure what to make of it. She wouldn't know he'd been born Ketchum but now went by Hollister.

Would she?

She returned her attention to Allie. "So what brings you to Lindell's? Your timing couldn't have been more crucial."

"Yeah," Jack growled, still testy over not being able to read her. "The more we stand here talking, the farther away Boone gets."

"Like Grace said, we need a plan," Mick said. "Maybe we should get the police involved again. Doesn't make sense to go tearing off into the hills like our tails were on fire. We spent a week with the posse doing just that, with no luck."

"But now we know they're close," Jack said firmly. "It'll be easier."

"My father is supposed to return today," Allie said. "That's why we rode into Great Falls this morning, to meet his train. Maybe he'll have some more information. His letter said he'll be accompanied by the private investigator he's hired for the case."

"He's been doing a fine job keeping in touch with George," Jack said, thinking of the photograph he'd seen at the police station.

"We stopped at Margaret's Eatery for a hot drink after the ride in," Mick added. "Saw Camille. She told us you were still in town and that you'd be bringing Grace out to the ranch to see Allie. Glad we got here before you did."

Allie lifted her fingers to her hat. "Shall we take off our coats?"

"Feel free," Jack growled, growing impatient. "But Mick can leave his on. He's not staying."

"Neither am I," Grace said.

Jack swung toward her. "The hell you're not."

"I'm not going to stay behind and do nothing."

"How many times does Boone have to come after you before you realize he means you harm?" Jack grated.

"How many times must I tell *you* that I have to do everything I can to get the Society's money back and help prove Charles's guilt?" she shot back.

"Charles." Allie rolled her eyes in contempt. "I can't wait to see the man rot in jail."

Grace swung toward her. "Boone can help us get him there."

"How?" Jack asked.

She faced him. "When we find where he's hiding, I want you to use me as bait to lure him out."

Taken aback, Jack glowered. "Are you crazy?"

"Not at all. I'll approach him on the pretense of trying to be his friend. He needs someone to trust. He'll listen to me."

"Oh, Grace. Think of the danger," Allie said, clearly appalled.

"If anyone goes up there, trying to be his friend, it'll be me," Jack said.

And wouldn't the old man find *that* amusing? Jack, hobnobbing with an outlaw, if only on pretense.

Grace shook her head. "He'll never trust you, Jack."

"Seems to me his 'trust' is a moot point. We just need to find him and bring him in. The 'how' we do it is up to him. The trust is optional." As far as Jack was concerned, the discussion had come to an end. Grace's plan wasn't feasible, bordered on ridiculous, and he wasn't going to waste any more time on it. He headed toward his coat. "Mick, you coming with me?"

"Sure thing, Jack."

"We'll head to the livery first and get mounted up."

Anticipation flourished in his veins. The snow would make tracking the outlaw easier, and maybe, just maybe, it wouldn't be much longer before the mystery of the missing library money would be solved.

Then, once Boone was behind bars, Jack could finally lay Sam Ketchum's request to rest. He would've found the man who set him up.

Yet, as he busied himself buttoning his coat and pulling on his gloves, he delayed leaving for precious minutes, his urge to hold Grace in his arms running strong within him. To tell her goodbye and assure her he'd do all he could to make her life right again. But mostly, he'd kiss her long and hard and store all those kisses in his heart while he was gone, so they could warm his blood when he needed them most.

But of course, he didn't do any of those things. He didn't have the right. Not like Mick had with Allie. Because Grace would never have a part in his life.

He grabbed his Stetson from the hook, yanked open the door and left Lindell's.

And knew that Grace was watching him go.

"I can't believe I let you talk me into this," Allie muttered over her shoulder. She pulled her scarf higher over her chin. "Mick and Jack are going to skin us alive when they find out."

"Don't think of it." Grace pushed her own trepidation

aside, beat it down into submission and buried it. "What we're taking is a terrible risk, but a necessary one."

She kept one eye on the horse in front of her. Allethaire—Allie, Grace mentally corrected—was a far better horsewoman, and it was up to her to lead the way up the narrow path. Grace had ridden very little since she was a child, and she had done all she could do to stay in the saddle. That the terrain was icy, steep and strewn with rocks only made the journey more treacherous, and she clung desperately to the saddle horn to keep from falling.

"Do you still see them?" she asked to distract Allie from her complaining.

She kept her voice as low as she could. Here in the hills, beyond the city limits, the littlest sound carried, and she tensed at every crunch of her mount's iron hooves against the frozen ground.

"Yes, but it's getting harder to keep them in sight. They're riding away from us."

Grace grimaced. The tree line afforded them valuable cover while they kept parallel with Jack and Mick, but if the pair veered too far away, Grace and Allie would lose them. Unless they veered toward them to *stay* parallel, of course, but that would only force her and Allie out into the open and ensure their detection.

Grace had to avoid that at all costs. She *liked* having her skin about her.

Allie tossed Grace another frown over her shoulder. "Need I remind you it's going to be dark soon?"

"No, Allie. You needn't."

Grace was beginning to feel testy, too. She avoided looking at the sky again to see how far the sun had inched down to the horizon. It seemed they'd been riding forever. They hadn't, not really, but the last time she'd checked, the structures outside Great Falls had become much too small.

Now she couldn't see them at all.

Allie unexpectedly pulled up. The ground had leveled somewhat, and the profusion of evergreens had thinned enough so that Grace had room to halt beside her.

"I've lost them," Allie said, pointing to her left. "They were right over there. It looks like they've disappeared into a valley or something."

Grace strained to see signs of movement in the direction Allie indicated and failed to see anything. Tendrils of panic stirred in her stomach. She wasn't so naïve as to think they could find Boone and Carl's hideout on their own. They needed to piggyback on Jack and his ability to track just about anyone.

She hid her panic from Allie. "Valley or not, we'll have to hurry to catch up with them."

"No." Her nose red from the cold, Allie regarded Grace stubbornly. "We have to head back. If we get lost out here, we'll freeze to death trying to find our way home."

Grace shook her head. "We've come too far to give up. We'll be wasting every minute we've spent getting to this point, and—"

"Don't be ridiculous. Do you really think we'll find Boone before it gets dark? And if we don't, then what? Do you want to ride on this stupid mountain all night? When it's pitch-dark and bone-numbing cold?"

Grace didn't want to admit Allie was right. Not when her friend was no stranger to danger. By now Grace knew all about how Allie had faced it head-on when she shot Reggie, the leader of Boone and Carl's gang, less than two weeks ago, not far from the Wells Cattle Company, while defending Mick from certain death.

And if Allie was unwilling to face this kind of danger—trying to hunt down an outlaw under conditions like these—then Grace knew she should be unwilling, too.

Awash in indecision, she sighed and hated to see her plan fail. She didn't want to go back to Lindell's empty-handed, without Boone, without information, no farther ahead in her need to convict Charles or help Carl than she was when she arrived in Montana Territory.

Carl.

Her thoughts latched on to him. Her half brother. Her only kin. Worrisome thoughts of where he was now. With Boone? On this mountain? Or had he somehow seen the folly of his ways and left the area, contrite and determined to start over in a new life?

She could only hope. Would he even appreciate that she was trying to help him? Would he ever be convinced having Boone as an accomplice was oh, so wrong for him?

Merciful saints, she wished Jack was here. She needed his arms to warm her. The strength, too, that was so much a part of him. He helped her forget her worries about Carl and her fears of never finding the Society's money again. He made her think of things far more exciting and wickedly forbidden….

He'd get her home, too. As fast as they could, with unerring accuracy.

"Grace?" Allie reached over and covered her gloved hand with her own. "Let's go back, shall we?"

This time, she didn't hesitate. "All right."

"I do understand, you know," Allie said. "Everything you're going through."

Sincerity laced her soft-spoken words. Grace squeezed her hand and fought tears. "I just hope I'm doing the right thing for…for everyone."

"You are," she said firmly. "Just not for the reasons you think."

If it wasn't for the cold, Grace would've explored the comment. She wanted to hear more of Allie's perspective and compare it with her own. She longed to confide how doing the "right thing" could turn all wrong.

But the day wasn't getting any brighter, nor the air any warmer, and they were fast running out of time.

"I saw a stream not far from here," Grace said instead. "It'll take us down the mountain. Follow me this way."

She turned her mount in the opposite direction from where she last saw Jack and Mick heading. She hated leaving them behind as they rode farther away from Great Falls, deeper into the dark and cold, but she took consolation in that the men were far more experienced and much more prepared than she and Allie. Hadn't they returned only yesterday from riding with the posse? They knew exactly what they were doing.

Allie and Grace, not as much.

"I smell wood smoke." From behind Grace, Allie spoke suddenly. "There must be a cabin around here somewhere."

Grace couldn't see one, but she smelled smoke, too. Faint, but definite. Dare they go in search in hopes the person inside might have caught a glimpse of Boone or Carl?

Or could it be their hideout?

"Don't even think it," Allie said with uncanny perception. "Just keep heading toward that stream."

Grace did, but with great reluctance. Her horse seemed to know their destination; perhaps he smelled water nearby, but it wasn't long before he took them right to a narrow stream, its water glistening crisp and cold in the late afternoon sunlight.

Yet it was the man hunkered upstream that pushed her heart right into her throat.

Allie let out a small gasp; Grace's quick gesture held her to silence. Boone didn't know they were there. He stared into the water, his back to them, and though his horse nickered softly, sensing their presence, the outlaw's thoughts seemed to consume him. He didn't move.

"I'm going over there," Grace whispered.

Looking miserable, Allie bit her lip and nodded. To leave now, when the outlaw was close and unaware, was unthinkable. It was why they'd ridden all the way out here, after all.

So Grace could talk to Boone.

"Wait here." Grace fought down a strong urge to turn tail and run. "If something goes wrong, ride out of here as fast as you can."

It was better that way, they'd decided on the way out. Split up to save the other.

"Remember where we are. Remember every detail. You still have the gun Mick gave you, don't you?" Grace asked.

Allie reached inside her coat and pulled out it out. "Yes."

"Warn Jack with it, if it comes to that." Grace took solace that he was already on the mountain, somewhere fairly close with Mick. He'd come running if he heard a shot or two.

Allie's blue eyes shone with her worry. "Are you sure about all this, Grace?"

"Of course, I am." She kept her whisper confident even as she realized how much could go wrong. That Boone, no matter who he was, was a pure-blooded savage. "You want the Society's money back, don't you?"

"I don't think I care anymore." But her fingers curled

around the weapon, as if assuring herself she'd use it, no matter what.

"Well, I do. I care a lot."

"Be careful, Grace. Promise me you will."

Grace nodded. "You know what to do, same as I do."

She drew in a breath and gathered the reins into her hands. Nudging her horse forward, closer to the outlaw, she prayed she wouldn't get herself killed.

Chapter Twelve

A saddlebag lay on the ground, not far from the water's edge. One flap had flung open, and from inside, the corner of a piece of gold-colored paper lifted in the breeze.

Grace drew up alongside it and focused on Boone's back. He didn't seem to know she was there or that he'd even dropped the bag. His horse had wandered, too, reins dragging, to graze on a patch of brown grass not covered by snow.

Whatever Boone was doing engrossed him. Perhaps a fish he'd caught, or something he was cleaning. His rifle remained close to his side, within reach, and Grace took great care not to startle him.

She lingered in the saddle to collect her courage. She had to confront him. She *had* to. Too much time had passed. Too many people had been hurt. Too much hinged on getting the library money back—

Lightning quick, his arm snaked out for his rifle with more speed than any man should be capable of. He whirled toward her with a feral yell and a lethal aim, and Grace cried out in terror.

He should've fired. That he didn't left her quaking in relief.

He knelt on one knee and stared, clearly stunned to see her.

"Don't shoot me, Alexandre. I'm alone."

Her voice shook with the half-lie. He wouldn't be able to see Allie hidden in the trees, too far back to be of much protection, but there, nevertheless.

"You lie." His black eyes sliced through the air around them, as if he expected a mounted posse with guns blazing to appear at any moment.

"I'm glad I found you." She looped the reins around the saddle horn and dismounted as gracefully as her numb muscles allowed. She kept talking to encourage his distraction. "It's important that I see you again."

His gaze sliced back to her. "How did you find me?"

"Quite by accident, I assure you."

"It was Carl, wasn't it? He told you."

"Carl?" Taken aback, Grace shook her head. Why would he accuse her half brother of such a thing? Had they quarreled? As far as she could tell, it would be of no benefit for Carl to betray Boone. Not when each was as guilty of robbery as the other, and a host of other crimes as well. "No. I promise you. I haven't seen him since this morning."

Slowly Boone rose. His grip on the rifle lightened. He faced her with his feet spread and his gaze riveted. "What do you want?"

Despite his harsh demand, his voice sounded less antagonistic. Intense and riveting, his black eyes fastened over her, as if now that he was assured she came alone, she consumed his every thought.

She'd seen that look from men before. Appreciation and desire. It gave her power, that look. She seized it and hung on for the strength to do what she had to do.

"I brought you some food." She untied a woven bag from her saddle. "A little meat, bread, a few tins of fruit." She managed a smile. "Nut Cake."

His glance dropped to the bag, then lifted again. "Why?"

"You're hungry, Alexandre." She hesitated, knowing she was going to offend his volatile pride. "You've gotten much too thin since we last met. You need nourishment."

His tongue slid along his chapped lips. Again, that dark gaze locked over her. Again she saw the pain, like she had earlier, in her room at Lindell's. The agony he couldn't hide.

"Why should it matter to you about what I need?" he asked hoarsely.

She didn't dare move closer. Not yet. She eased the bag of food to the ground.

"Because you must go back to being Alexandre." Grace played her trump card and hoped she wasn't making the biggest mistake of her life. "It is who you are."

A tremor rolled through him.

"Admit it to me, Alexandre. You're not really Boone, are you? Deep in your heart? You hate being forced to live as him. Anyone would." She took courage from his tortured silence. "The man I met in Minneapolis wouldn't have fallen so low. What happened?"

"I do what I must."

"Why?"

"Because of the Cause, damn you!"

His snarl echoed through the hills. A breeze, stronger here, out of the tree line, plucked at her hair, tossing loose strands against her cheek where they caught at the corner of her mouth. Mindlessly she pulled them away.

"Your people." She recalled how he'd mentioned them before, at Lindell's.

"Yes." He gritted the word.

"They're suffering?"

"They are *oppressed,* Grace. They are poor and hungry. They have no home, no hope."

The admission held her riveted. She felt as if he'd dragged her to the edge of something immense, more complex, than she could have imagined.

Yet she suspected he shared this hidden part of himself with her as he'd shared with no other. Including Carl, who never gave her any indication of a cause to steal money for, except the one of his own foolish greed.

Would Charles be in on Boone's secret?

Grace was convinced he was.

Now Boone gave her an opportunity to glimpse a side of Charles he'd never before shared in the time she'd known him, or worked with him, and her heart pounded in trepidation of all she might see....

"Who are your people, Alexandre?" she asked softly.

His shoulders squared with the pride that drove him. "We are Métis."

"In America?"

"In Canada." His lip curled with contempt, and she knew her ignorance wasn't lost on him.

"Yet you fight for them here?"

"We must."

"With money you *steal* from us?"

The accusation was out before she could catch herself, and he stiffened. "I do not expect you to understand."

"But I do. More than you know."

She had Bess Reilly to thank for enlightening her. Along with the Ketchum gang, her mother stole untold thousands of dollars for the mere thrill of the crime with no thought of the people she hurt. Her life never improved from all that money. The opposite, in fact.

She'd paid the ultimate price, at a terrible cost to the family she left behind.

But Grace didn't understand why Carl was part of the scheme. What would he know of these people, the Métis? Why would he care? As far as she knew, he'd never crossed America's northern border or had reason to be involved in Canada's political strife.

A gust of wind whipped through the hillside and slapped her with a harsh reminder of the deepening chill. Daylight was fast fading, and she'd yet to uncover the truth she craved most. The location of the stolen money.

She took a breath. "Is Charles Métis, too, Alexandre?"

Boone stood, unmoving. Just stared at her with those fierce black eyes, bloodshot from fatigue, and the hate and resentment simmering inside him. He seemed oblivious to the cold, and Grace found it frightening he could be so unfeeling. So driven with no thought of himself.

His silence unnerved her, and the first stirrings of fear crept into her awareness. Maybe she'd been wrong to come all the way out here to use herself as bait, attempting to win his trust so that he'd reveal the whereabouts of the Society's stolen money. Maybe she should've trusted Jack to solve the case his own way. She already knew his reputation as a shrewd lawman, one of the best.

A piece of gold paper somersaulted toward her, plucked by the wind from the open saddlebag nearby.

The sight of it distracted her for a moment, and she almost bent to save it from being blown away.

Until she reminded herself she couldn't take her eyes off Boone and the weapon he wielded.

"Go on, Grace," he said softly. He sauntered toward her, one step, then another and another. "Pick it up. Read what it says. Then you'll know the truth about Charles Renner."

Her heart tattooed against her chest. His mockery unleashed her insecurities, freeing them to rush forward and remind her of the all the times she'd struggled to keep from looking stupid. From *feeling* stupid, most of all.

He growled from her dawdling. "Pick it up, I said."

The coward in her refused, compelled by the personal secret she was loathe to expose, now of all times. "Why don't you tell me what it says, Alexandre?"

The paper tumbled between them, and he caught it from rolling past with a quick stomp of his boot.

"Don't play games with me, woman."

Grace didn't dare test his patience further, and reluctantly she bent and pulled the note out from beneath his boot sole. She straightened again, brushing away bits of snow with her gloved fingers.

"What is this?" She stalled for the time her brain needed. "A telegram?"

She raised the paper, then lowered it, pretending she needed better light in the gathering dusk.

SLCNE HRE RFO GODO. LD

SILCNE RHE RFO GOOD. DL

Grace squinted, straining hard to read the letters jumping back and forth with a life of their own, until they fell together in proper order.

SILENCE HER FOR GOOD. LD

Oh, God.

A crippling mix of horror and anguish choked her. She swayed. "What kind of sick joke is this?"

Boone stood in front of her. So close he could reach out and grab her by the throat. Tiny ice crystals sprinkled his dark beard and moustache. She smelled the stench on him. The lust. His eyes glinted like black diamonds, hard and bright.

"Charles doesn't want you around anymore, Grace," he purred. "And if your grandmother hadn't died first, he would've killed her, too."

Pain seared Grace's breast, into her heart. All those months he'd worked with the Ladies Literary Aid Society, with Lucille Reilly at the helm, Grace at her side, he'd been plotting to *kill* them?

"I don't believe you," she said.

But deep down, she did. Because now, everything made sense. The scandal and ruination of their library plans, the embezzled money planted in Allie's trunk, setting her up for robbery, all for the sake of his cause.

All that remained was seeing them dead.

How could she have been so blind?

"I know him far better than you ever did, Grace," Boone taunted. "I don't care if you believe me or not."

His arrogance stung. She scrambled to corral her self-pity and reclaim her pride. Charles didn't know of the papers she'd brought with her, the evidence she intended to find with Allie to incriminate him.

"You're right, Alexandre." It took all her willpower to keep her voice steady and her chin up. To keep the game going, so she could win. "Charles is far away. Let's forget him for now. It's *you* I'm here to talk about. Not him."

A pathetic hunger flickered in his expression, and he dismissed the disturbing telegram with appalling ease. He stepped closer, his hand outstretched, as if he intended to take hold of her arm. "You're very beautiful, Grace. Did Charles ever tell you how beautiful you are?"

The last time Boone had told her that, he'd almost kidnapped her. Grace stepped back, putting as much space between them as she dared. "No. Nor did he tell me what a terrible friend he is to you." *To both of us.* She clucked her tongue in disgust. In broiling hurt. "Expecting you to live like an outcast while he enjoys the life of the privileged. He conspires with you to steal money, yet it's *you* the law is after, while he hides behind his powerful alibis in Minneapolis. Protected and safe."

Boone's nostrils flared.

"Let me be your friend, Alexandre." She forced herself to say the words. Not that she was so naive to think he'd reveal the location of the Society's funds, but garnering his trust would be the first crucial step.

She hoped. "Take the food I bring you. Will you do that for me?"

He appeared to fight an inner war. "This kindness you show me—"

"Is just that. Kindness. Nothing more."

She had to build his trust, little by little, for him to believe it was real. Emboldened by his silence, she turned back toward the bag of food she'd left on the ground...and spied Jack crouched behind a jutting snow-covered rock, with his gun leveled at Boone's back. Grace couldn't see Mick, couldn't know where he might be, but her heart pounded from what would happen when Boone learned they'd come.

She couldn't feast her eyes on Jack or let him know how glad she was he was here. She didn't dare lest Boone see him, too. Did Jack have any idea of the mess she'd put herself in? That she had no idea how to get out?

Her mount snuffled and pranced. Boone froze at the horse's nervousness. His dark gaze whipped around in suspicion.

Grace quickly hefted the bag to turn his attention back to her. "Please, Alexandre. Take this, and then I'll leave. It's gotten terribly late, and—"

A gunshot thundered through the mountain. Boone's lips pulled back in a snarl; he snatched the rifle to his shoulder.

But it wasn't Jack he aimed at, but the rider barreling down the hill at breakneck speed, so unruly, so thoughtless of the ice and snow, the very real possibility his mount could slip and fall and kill them both.

Carl. Oh, *Carl*. Crazy wild as always and riding straight toward Jack with a revolver in one hand, the reins gripped in the other.

"You ready to die, Jack Ketchum?" he yelled. "'Cuz you're gonna, y'hear? You're gonna *die right now*."

Jack rose up from behind the rock. Fearless and powerful and hauntingly calm, he extended his arm and aimed his gun with a steady hand. He bided his time, defying the certainty of the bullet. Defying death. Giving Carl precious seconds to change his mind and keep from killing a man in cold blood.

Grace screamed. Jack's name or Carl's, she didn't know. But her heart pounded in terror for the man who would fire too late and inevitably breathe his last…

The shots came, a split second apart, shattering the mountain's stillness and yanking time hideously still.

Jack's arm lowered.

Carl's body jerked. His wild expression contorted in shock. The revolver fell from his grip, then the reins, and he dropped from the saddle with a sickening thud.

Suddenly time began to race, too fast to stop, instilling Grace with the horrible knowledge that she would never get back what she was about to lose. That too much time had been wasted, had been taken for granted, and it was all her fault. It would always be her fault.

Grace broke into a run toward Carl, a tiny part of her realizing that Boone had begun to run, too. From somewhere above her, or behind her, another shot rang out. Somewhere in the trees, or maybe from the rocky outcropping, but it didn't matter what was happening. What Jack yelled, or Mick, or where Boone was headed. Whose horse clamored over the snow or whose bolted into the mountain stream, splashing clear, icy water in his wake.

Only Carl mattered, and she dropped to her knees beside him. An awful gurgling sound pushed from his throat, and she ripped his coat open to help him breathe.

"You stupid fool!" She choked the words out, past her sobs, an overwhelming grief for her troublemaking half brother tearing through her. "What were you thinking?"

"Gracee." His lashes fluttered open, then closed. "You were always as slow...as a snail on a greased log." He wheezed a cackle, amused even now. Like this. "So I...had to do the killin' for us."

Nausea churned in her belly, but she forced it back. "Hush, Carl." Blood trickled out from his mouth, down his chin. She swiped at it with her glove, making the ugliness go away. The violence that was so much a part of him. "Don't try to talk."

"Ma did love you." He drew in a rattled breath. "Jus' so you know."

Grace fell still. "What?"

"You were her...little china doll." His eyes opened,

and his mouth formed a weak grin. "That's what she used to call you."

"No." Riveted, Grace shook her head. "Never—I never heard her say that."

"She did." He grimaced against the pain. "'Cuz you wasn't…tough like us."

Hot tears burned her eyes. She pressed her fingers to her lips to hold in a sob. "Mama said that about me?"

He gagged on the blood. Didn't answer for oh, so long.

"Yeah," he said finally, his eyes struggling to stay open. "Lots of times."

"Oh, Carl." Tears spilled over and streamed down her cheeks.

"That's why she sent you away. She wanted you to live like…a true lady. 'Cuz that's what you were."

Grace couldn't speak. Too much of her was dying inside, right along with Carl.

"She loved you. Always…meant to tell you, y'know?" He sucked in air. "But, Gracee?"

His voice had fallen perilously weak, and she huddled over him so she could hear.

"I'm not…goin' to tell you…where we hid the money."

Her head jerked up. His jaw sagged. The wheezing fell silent. And as fast as that, he was gone.

"Grace." Hasty steps crunched snow behind her. Lean fingers grasped her by the shoulders and pulled her aside. Jack sounded grim. "Let me see what I can do for him."

Fueled by the hurt and anguish raging through her, Grace swung toward him and flailed her fists against his chest. "You killed him! Damn you, Jack! You killed him!"

He grabbed her wrists, held them hard. "He didn't give me a choice. You know he didn't."

"You've taken everyone from me now, haven't you?" The accusations flew free, hurled from a terrible pain deep inside her. "I'll never forgive you. Never, ever!"

Slender arms pulled her from him. Allie, in all her compassion and understanding. "She's distraught, Jack. She doesn't mean what she's saying."

"Can you get her home for us?" Mick's voice was as grim as Jack's. "We have to take care of matters here."

"Yes, of course. I know the way."

"Help me get her on her horse." Jack took her again, bundled her tight against him, yet Grace was past caring. Beyond thinking. Too emotionally drained to fight him again.

But after he lifted her into the saddle, after she and Allie began their ride down the hill and back to Lindell's, Grace knew her time for revenge had come.

Chapter Thirteen

She waited for Jack to come.

He would, of course. They had unfinished business. He'd want to know why she defied his orders and conspired with Allie to track down Boone. It wouldn't even matter they overcame the risks and succeeded. He'd only care that Boone had gotten away, taking the location of the stolen money with him.

Again.

Grace took another sip of wine. Warmth slid down to her belly, through her blood and numbed her pain.

Jack would want to know how she was doing, too. She wouldn't tell him that it took her half brother's dying for her to learn the one thing about her mother she would always treasure: that Bess had loved her in her own way. But why did Carl's death have to be the price she had to pay to hear it?

Still, she couldn't deny Jack's concern would be genuine. He was a hard man, but not an indifferent one. Grace had only to think of the passion in his kisses, the hunger in his gray-green eyes whenever he looked at her, to know he wasn't immune to her.

Far from it.

He wouldn't expect her to want to kill him, though, and that would be her biggest advantage. One she had to use at the perfect moment. When he least expected it.

The fire in the grate snapped and hissed. Grace sat cross-legged on the bed and absorbed the flickering heat. She had no idea how late it was, only that darkness had long since fallen. Even so, she hadn't bothered to light the lamp on the bureau; her morose thoughts were better suited to a shadowed room than a well-lit one.

He'd be here anytime. She could hear the low rumble of his voice downstairs, making his goodbyes to Mick and Allie before they left for Paris Gibson's apartment, where they intended to spend the night.

By the time Grace refilled her glass, the voices had quieted, the door had been pushed closed, and footsteps ascended the stairs.

One after the other they came, down the hall, closer to her room. Her gaze dropped to the threshold, to the shadows planted beneath the door, on the other side.

Though she expected his knock, the firm sound of it rattled the quiet of her room. Rattled *her.* She threw back a little more wine to calm her nerves, drew in a breath and set the glass aside.

"Come in, Jack."

The door eased open, and there he was. All six foot plus two inches of him, pure muscle and power and so much damned virility her mouth up and dried.

His glance took in the darkened room. The half-empty bottle on the bedside table. Her. She imagined how she must look to him, sitting here on the red-and-brown checkered quilt with her hair loose and still damp from washing, and dressed in her nightclothes. It wasn't proper for a lady to invite a man into her room when she looked like this, but then, this was a night unlike any other, wasn't it?

A corner of his mouth lifted. "How'd you know it was me?"

"I've been expecting you."

He took a step inside, closed the door behind him. He filled the place with his presence, consumed her senses, her every thought.

"Then you'll know why I'm here." He came closer, but halted at the foot of the bed.

She cocked her head and regarded him with a cool look. "To see to my, oh, so tender sensibilities?"

A muscle in his jaw moved. "That, and to clear up a thing or two between us."

"Meaning Carl and Boone."

"You decide which one we'll talk about first."

"Hmm." She tucked long strands of hair behind her

ear. "Let's see. Since you killed him tonight, let's start with Carl."

He wasn't amused by her sarcasm. "What the *hell* did you expect me to do, Grace? Let him come at me, screaming like a banshee?"

"Spare his life, for starters."

"When he had no intention of sparing mine?"

"You didn't have to shoot him dead, Jack!"

"Yes. I did." Raw fury emanated from him. He leaned forward; her gaze followed him down. He braced both hands on the quilt and snared her with a hard look. "You knew him, didn't you?"

The secrets she'd kept for so long started to slip out of her grasp. Like they were greased in butter. Little by little, until she could no longer hold on to them.

"Yes," she said.

"Who is he?"

She shouldn't be so afraid to let the secrets go and let Jack know who she really was. It was all part of the plan, after all. To throw the humiliating truth at him, so she could kill him.

"Were you in on the embezzling scheme with them, Grace?" he taunted.

She jerked back. "That's ridiculous."

"Were you working with Carl and Boone so you could have a cut of the loot? I'll bet you're not really with the Ladies Literary Aid Society, either. Am I right, honey? You're really part of their gang."

Maybe she shouldn't have been insulted at the

accusation. But she was. Her bosom lifted from growing outrage.

"No, I'm not, and you know it!" she snapped.

"Then who the hell is Carl?" Jack roared.

"He's my brother, damn you! My brother."

If Grace had reached out and slapped him, Jack couldn't have looked more stunned.

"Your brother?" he choked.

"*Half* brother."

"What's his name?"

"Reilly." She strove for the composure she desperately needed to see her plan through. "Carl Reilly."

Jack stared at her, as if she'd sprouted a second nose.

Then, abruptly, he pushed off the mattress and swung away from her, raking a hand through his hair, trying to make sense of it all. Grace reached behind the pillow and curled her fingers around cold metal.

Jack paced the short length of her room to the wall. "He knew who I was." He swung back toward her. "How did he know I was Jack Ketchum?"

She whipped out the revolver and gripped it in both hands.

She didn't need to say anything more.

Jack dropped his glance to the Derringer and gritted a terse oath. In the firelight, the scar slashing his cheek turned his features hard and cruel. The imposing breadth of his shoulders, his ability to fill the room with his power, his burgeoning fury, transformed him into a warrior who would fight until he could fight no more.

He frightened her, standing there. As capable of destroying her as she was of him.

"I'll tell you once, and once only, to put that gun down," he said.

She shivered at the lethal calm in his voice. "I'm going to kill you, Jack."

"Oh?" He arched his brow and took a lazy step toward her. "Was it something I said?"

"Something you did, and don't move any closer."

"Something I did." As if she'd never spoken, he moved again. Easily. "Care to enlighten me?"

"Not only did you kill my brother, but you killed my mother, too."

He froze in midstep. "The hell I did."

"Bess Reilly, remember? In New Mexico Territory, a year ago."

"Sweet saints in heaven."

"She rode with the Ketchum gang. Sam and Black Jack and the others."

He went still. Deathly still.

"She was *there,* Jack. When you and your blood-thirsty posse tracked them down." To Grace's horror, her chin trembled, and her eyes welled up with tears. But the grip on her revolver never wavered. "She died, like a hunted animal. She never saw you before, or any of the men with you, but you killed her anyway."

A deep, primal sound erupted from his throat. Grace

had barely registered the ferocity of it, that it had come from somewhere inside of him so full of anger, so shredded with pain, when he came at her. A mind-numbing blur of man and muscle and cunning speed.

She was no match for the sheer heaviness of him. He threw his body against hers, tackling her sideways on the bed, his hand fast against her wrist. She cried out her surprise, her frustration and pain from the viselike grip of his fingers. A grip so strong he could break each slender bone if he wanted.

And he would, if she didn't give in. Yet Grace hung on to the Derringer as long as she could, until it hurt too much, and her grasp helplessly weakened. He snatched the revolver, and she curled away from him, into the pillows, giving into tears of anguish, of abject failure and loss, freeing them all from her broken heart.

Behind her came the metal-against-metal sound of bullets pulled crisply from their chamber. Then, the mattress shifted, Jack murmured her name, and he pulled her toward him, into his arms, until the sobs quieted.

Grace lay on her back beneath him and sniffled. She refused to look at him at first, not while she warred with a bevy of emotions, turned topsy-turvy from the wine in her blood and the confusion he always made her feel.

He drew the side of his hand over her wet cheek, wiping away the heaviest of her tears with a touch so gentle, she welled up all over again.

"Damned if I'm going to let you blame me for Bess's death, Grace." His voice carried a thread of resolve, but desperation, too. "I've never bragged to be perfect, but the only person I killed that day was…my father."

Even before she spoke the words, she realized how they'd sound coming out of her mouth. That she was grasping at straws, that she wasn't being fair, that she didn't hate Jack as much as she thought. Or should.

But she had to say them anyway, because they needed to be said. He had to know he'd destroyed her family, one after the other, leaving her alone. Forever alone.

She owed it to Carl. To Bess. But mostly, she owed it to herself.

Her gaze didn't waver. "You were the last man standing, Jack."

His brow knitted. "And that makes me guilty?"

"Who else can I blame?" Her chin quivered anew. It wasn't right for either of them, her heart insisted. Not anymore. Not like it used to be, but still she clung to the belief he was responsible. "Everyone died in that shoot-out. No one else can be accountable, can they?"

"It wasn't my bullet, Grace!"

"Does it have to be?"

"Hell, yes!" His hand fisted near her ear. "If you're going to hold me responsible, then at least have it be when I pulled the trigger."

"Maybe you did."

"Only once. And not at her." His jaw moved. "It wasn't like you think. I swear."

He was right, of course. Tonight, she'd clung to a fantasy formed from sketchy information about her mother's killing. Goaded by Carl's misguided hate, she'd blown it up in her mind, allowed it to fester…until she'd almost made a terrible mistake.

She would've been no better than her mother.

No better than Carl.

A murderer, of the worst degree.

She drew in a miserable, weepy breath.

"Did Carl put you up to your scheme to kill me?" he asked roughly.

"No." She trembled at the memory of her brother's terrible vengeance, halted only by a split-second of fate. "He wanted the pleasure all for himself."

"So where'd you get the gun?"

"It's Allie's. She got it from Mick," she said in a small voice, enduring a new round of guilt that she'd taken it without her friend's knowledge. Something Grace had every intention of rectifying the moment she saw Allie again. "I've never owned a weapon in my life."

Jack regarded her, his features solemn, as if he tried to decide if she spoke the truth.

"Nor have I ever belonged to a gang," she added stiffly. "Don't you dare accuse me of it again."

"No." He conceded with a slow nod. "It's not your style."

Her style?

She didn't know what her style could be, unless, perhaps, it was her maddening inability to know the truth in the people she loved most. Their honesty and integrity. Or the lack of it.

"For what it's worth, Grace," Jack said quietly. "I'm sorry about Carl."

She swallowed. Hard. "He was trouble from the day he was born."

"But he was still your brother."

"Yes, he was that."

"And Bess, too." Jack paused, and Grace sensed he was thinking of her mother, of that horrific day when so many on both sides of the law had died. "I wish things could've been different for all of us."

"Me, too," she whispered in a wobbly voice, yearning—as she always would—for the normal, law-biding family she never had.

Regardless, losing her mother had been difficult; her grandmother doubly so. But Carl's death drove home the devastating reality that Grace had failed to save him. In spite of everything she'd done, or tried to do, he'd died too young, too violently.

He didn't need her anymore.

No one did.

A new round of tears she could no more halt than she could fly to the moon spilled out of the corners of her eyes. Another outpouring of sadness for what would never be…

"Grace, honey." Jack smoothed her hair with slow, gentle strokes. "Reckon you're feeling about as low as anyone can get about now. But for what it's worth to you, I'm here. And I'm not leaving until you feel better."

She wanted him to go.

She wanted him to stay.

Mostly she wanted him to hold her.

"You d-don't have to be nice to me, you know." She hiccupped. "I just tried to shoot you dead."

"Yeah, I know." His thumb stopped a stream of tears and wiped them away. "I'm not real happy about that, but I guess I'll have to forget about it for now."

"I'm sorry." She breathed in deep, let the air out slow. A shred of composure returned. "Really, Jack. I am."

"You owe me, woman."

"You don't have to tell me how much."

He'd been nothing short of the perfect gentleman from the time she'd first met him. Strong and protective, compassionate and kind. What had she done to acknowledge that, but reward him with suspicion and the worst kind of betrayal?

"Can you ever forgive me?" The plea rushed out of her mouth in abject humility. In the purest of sincerity. "If you can't, I'll understand, but I'm hoping you'll at least consider it."

"I'm considering, all right." The gray in his eyes darkened. His voice turned husky. "Lots of ways to make me forgive you."

His meaning wasn't lost on her, and her pulse skipped a beat. The air between them shifted, and suddenly everything started to change, twisting into a keen awareness of what it was like to lay on the bed like this. Together. Just the two of them in her room.

It didn't matter how it happened, or why. Grace knew

only that she needed to be with him. She wanted him…
she refused to rationalize her yearning, growing stronger
with every pulsing beat of her heart. Later, she would.
She'd have to. But for now, she could think only of Jack,
that he was very much alive. Vibrant and real. Her hand
lifted, and she laid her palm across his scarred cheek,
the part of him that she admired…and made him different in so many ways from other men she'd known.

"Stay with me tonight," she whispered.

His head angled, and he pressed a tender kiss to the
inside of her wrist. "Don't think you could keep me
away, honey."

The words filled her with heady triumph, and she
slid her hand under the collar of his shirt. So warm, his
neck. So strong, too. She pulled him down for his kiss,
her lips parting in readiness for their intoxicating feel.

She didn't expect their gentleness. Their playful
seduction. Not after he'd kissed her with such fierce
possessiveness only this morning. Jack Hollister was a
hard man, and he'd kissed like one.

But not now. Not this time.

His teeth nipped and teased and flirted with her lower
lip, then her upper one. His tongue leisurely traced the
shape of her mouth, back and forth, until he left her lips
wet and aching.

And curving in amusement at how he masterfully
plied them, bringing her to the brink of a full-fledged
kiss, then pulling back, denying her.

"What is this little tête-à-tête you do, Jack Hollister?"

she whispered coyly. "I fear the rules are too difficult to play."

She turned her head, giving him no access to the mouth he gave sport to, but danced around. His chuckle sounded low and deliciously pleasing in her ear.

"My rules, yes. Meant to break and enjoy." He dropped sensuous nibbles along the curve of her neck, raising gooseflesh clear to her toes. He took her lobe between his teeth and nibbled there, too.

But when his head lifted, his amusement had faded.

"By the time I'm done with you, Grace, you're not going to remember anything or anyone, y'hear?" He fisted his hands into her hair. His gaze drifted over her face. "Except me and the love we've made."

She'd not often seen him look so intense, or speak so fervently, and her skin tingled in excitement.

He pushed away from her, and the mattress lifted from the absence of his weight. There seemed to be no need for words while he made short work of removing his gunbelt, unbuttoning his shirt and Levi's, of pulling off his boots and woolen socks, then his knitted union suit. With every layer of clothing he peeled from his body, her breathing quickened and her anticipation heightened.

Merciful saints, he was a fine sampling of man. What woman wouldn't want to give herself completely to him? Tall and lean, every muscle honed taut, his skin golden in the firelight, he was manhood at its finest. His buckskin hair hung shiny and thick to his shoulders, and he carelessly swept it all back before he lowered himself over her again.

"You have any idea how many times I've thought of doing what I'm about to do to you right now?" he murmured, tugging the satin ribbon belt of her nightgown free.

His fingers seemed too thick to manage the tiny pearl buttons, but he undid them with ease, and moving with lazy deliberation, as if he savored every fractured second of what was to come, he parted the Wedgewood blue cotton wide.

The room's fire-warmed air touched her naked breasts, her belly, her thighs, and she trembled from lying before him like this. He drew in a ragged breath… and feasted a long, hungry gaze over her.

"Perfect," he whispered huskily. "Just as perfect as I knew you'd be."

If she could speak, she would've denied it. She'd made far too many mistakes, been responsible for too many failures, had believed and betrayed wrongly too many times to ever deserve the praise.

Yet the feel of his hands spanning her waist dashed any semblance of logical thought or conversation. Roughened by work, capable of killing a man or gentling a woman, they slid reverently upward over her ribs with luscious seduction toward the mounds of flesh all but quivering to be claimed….

He held one in each palm as if they were precious

gold, and lowered his head, taking a hardened nipple into the heat of his mouth. Grace sucked in a breath at the exquisite sensation and speared her fingers into his hair, holding him to her while his tongue lavished her with sweet torture. And when he repeated the seduction on the other side, she knew she was lost.

Lost to the mastery of an outlaw's son who made her feel cherished as a woman. Who didn't care who she was or what she'd done. Who didn't know all her imperfections and likely wouldn't care if he did.

He swept her away, up into the clouds, to places she'd never been. Somehow, at some moment, her nightgown landed in a lacy blue heap on the floor, over his Levi's and boots and holstered guns. Their bodies turned into a tangle of naked skin. Of clinging arms and legs. Of frenzied desire and whispered words meant only for each other.

With Jack, there was no inhibition, only shared intimacies and unquestioned trust. Grace gave him her body while she helped herself to his. He taught her deliciously wicked pleasures she never before imagined….

When the fire raged too hot between them, when the time had come to climb high and be quenched, he rose above her, a sheen of perspiration on his sleek, muscled body, bulging from restraint. Her thighs parted wide, and he probed the petals of her femininity. He found his place inside her with one slick thrust, and her back arched with a gasp.

"Grace," he rasped. "Sweet, perfect Grace."

He filled her with their coupling and rocked her with his loving. With each timeless thrust, they climbed higher and higher, past the clouds and into the sky, and together, as one, they reached their climax and shattered into a million glorious stars.

Chapter Fourteen

A Redheaded Woodpecker tap-tap-tapped against a barren branch outside Grace's window. Jack figured the little critter got separated from the rest of his family somehow and wound up in Great Falls to spend his winter. Not that he seemed bothered by it; he cheerfully flitted from branch to branch, offering a welcome spot of color under the morning sun.

Just like Grace brought into Jack's life.

Color, pleasure and happiness. Fulfillment. Their loving had been…incredible. So much so they'd turned to each other again in the night to sate the fiery need burning in their blood.

Only to find the fire unquenchable.

Jack dropped a kiss into her hair, a mass of shining sable pooling over his arm and against the stark-white pillow. He relished the feel of her warm, naked body cocooned against his while she slept. Waking up with his thigh on hers, her ankle curled around his calf while his palm cradled the delectable weight of her breast… hell, it felt right to be with her like this.

Perfect and right.

He'd fallen in love with her. Crazy hard in love. From the moment he first laid eyes on her, the Lady in Blue sitting all alone in Margaret's Eatery had stolen his heart.

Last night had only confirmed how much he wanted her in his life. And what the hell was he going to do about it?

One thing he knew for sure. He didn't know how he was going to let her go back to Minneapolis. And she would, after they found the Society's stolen money. She had friends there. Her obligation to see the library finished. It was a life that would have no place for a scar-faced lawman-turned-cowboy, as imperfect as she was perfect.

Once she opened those striking blue eyes of hers, things would look a lot different than they did last night, when her emotions had been raw from the effects of wine, her brother's death and, Jack knew, her determination to kill him.

He took comfort in knowing she didn't want him dead. At all. Grieving, hurting, she'd lashed out, but Jack had had enough experience with women to know when intimacy was real, when it wasn't, and last night,

Grace had made love with a fervency that almost melted his bones.

Still, she'd always associate him with her mother's death. He understood that. Accepted it. It had been his posse who'd gunned the gang down, and yeah, he was the last man standing. The only one left to take the blame.

A troubled sigh escaped him, and his breath fluttered the strands of soft hair at her temple. As if she sensed the way of his thoughts, Grace stirred. Her lashes slowly lifted, and Jack endured the bite of regret that their time in bed was about to end.

Her dark head rolled on the pillow. She blinked up at him, and a languid smile curved her full mouth. The mouth he'd explored and tasted and tantalized again and again through the night.

"What time is it?" she asked, her soft voice husky from slumber.

"Late. Very late."

"Mmm. Too bad." Rustling the covers, she shifted from one side to the other and stretched, like a lazy, pampered cat. She slid her arms around his neck and pressed her warm, silken body against him with the grace and ease of a woman who was right where she wanted to be. And had no intention of leaving anytime soon. "Let's stay here forever, shall we?"

The pebbled tips of her breasts against his chest gave him an inkling of her thinking; his blade thickened and throbbed with familiar yearning.

"Don't ask me twice, woman," he murmured, his hand finding one slim buttock. He helped himself to an appreciative squeeze. "You'll convince me for sure."

She purred, as if the ache in his response pleased her. "Forever and ever and ever, Jack."

She slid her tongue into the hollow of his throat. Licked and swirled and nuzzled him in blatant invitation to give her what she wanted.

What they both wanted.

And though it took every shred of willpower he possessed, Jack couldn't.

He reluctantly, but firmly, pulled her arms from around him and eased her back onto the mattress. Still, unable to leave her just yet, he succumbed to the need to taste her again, and he took her mouth in a hungry, fiercely controlled kiss that begged to prolong their time together, if only for a few minutes more.

When his head lifted, his blood had warmed up again, and her breathing turned ragged.

He forced himself to move away and resettle the blankets over her. Robbed of the heat of her body, gooseflesh raised on his naked skin.

"I'll build up the fire," he said. "It's as cold as a witch's tits in here."

Amusement from his crudity grew into tinkling laughter when he cursed mightily at the sensation of the frigid floor against his bare feet. He worked quickly to throw more wood into the block and poke the embers to life, and in short time, a healthy fire flared again.

Grace sat up and pulled her knees to her chest, keeping the covers close about her.

"What now, Jack?" She watched him tug on his socks, then reach for his knitted union suit. "Where do we go from here?"

Jack wasn't sure if she was preparing to leave him so soon—or if she meant their investigation into the stolen money.

He chose the safer of the two.

"It's only right that we see to the remains of your brother. He deserves a decent burial." Though Jack wasn't entirely convinced he did, but for Grace's sake, he'd make sure the kid got one. "Then we meet with Paris. I'm hoping he'll have information to share with us."

She frowned. "That would be good."

"Better than good. It's imperative."

"I just want this whole thing to be over with."

Grace flung back the covers and slid out of the sheets. Jack buttoned his Levi's and reached for his shirt. His gaze clung to her creamy nakedness and the graceful way her body moved, a perfect synchronization of female hips and arms and legs. Without a shred of shyness from his staring.

But then, why would she be shy? He'd already seen and tasted every beautiful inch of her.

"It will end, Grace. Soon enough."

Jack couldn't bring himself to agree with her about wanting the case closed. Not when a part of him wanted it to go on forever. As long as it did, she'd be here with him, trying to solve it, too.

Grace strode toward the bureau and pulled open the top drawer, bringing out a fresh chemise. On the bureau's surface lay a wad of gold-colored paper she'd obviously crumpled and tossed aside.

Part of the words were visible. Recognizable. The bold, black letters declaring *The Western Union Telegraph Company.*

"What's this?" he asked, the urge running strong in him to pick up the telegram and read what it said. He needed to know who sent it. And when. Mostly he wanted to know why she hadn't mentioned it to him.

Her head popped out above the neckline of her white cotton undergarment; she straightened the fabric around her hips. "What's what?" Seeing what he indicated, she paled. "Oh. That. I meant to throw it away."

She reached for it.

He clamped her wrist, preventing her.

His mind rolled to last night when he and Mick spied Grace and Allie following them on the mountain, in the tree line. They'd circled back and found Grace off her horse, talking to Boone. She'd picked something up from the snow. A piece of gold paper. It took her some time to read it, and whatever it said upset her.

"Why did Boone want you to read the telegram?" he demanded in a rough voice.

She bit her lip. "Because it was about me."

"You?" *That* he hadn't expected. "Who sent it?"

"I'm not sure."

It wasn't easy, but he reined in his burgeoning suspicions. As far as he knew, wires were always signed, but maybe this one wasn't. "I want to know what it says."

"Jack." She angled her gaze sideways. Since he still held her wrist, she couldn't walk away. "Please. Not now."

One-handed, he smoothed out the wad and thrust it at her. He could read the wire himself; the words were right there. One easy glance. She wouldn't be able to stop him.

But her evasiveness troubled him. What didn't she want him to know?

"It's only one sentence, Grace," he growled. "Read it for me."

She turned back. Her chin lifted; her throat worked. Pain welled in her ocean-blue eyes.

What wasn't she telling him?

"I can't," she said quietly.

"You can't?" he shot back. "Or won't?"

But before he could bite back the words, a startling possibility emerged from hers.

Images popped into Jack's mind…Grace at the restaurant, poring over the menu with her fingertip sliding slowly—painstakingly—across the page…

"I *can*." Sounding miserable, she corrected herself. "But not easily and not particularly well."

The note Carl had given her at the woodshed came, too, reminding Jack how he'd conveniently informed her of its contents. An image of the Nut Cake she'd made, without a cookbook in sight, followed…

"So read it yourself, if you want." Her voice kicked an octave higher. Beneath the chemise's thin cotton, her bosom lifted. "I don't care."

And yet another one dropped into his memory. On the mountain last night, while she stalled for time with Boone's note in her hand…

"Do you hear me, Jack?" She sounded ready to crack from his ruminating. Which was growing more enlightened by the moment.

She stood as still as stone, looking up at him with pain and anguished pride in her eyes, as if she braced for the recrimination she was sure would come.

But wouldn't. Not from him. Not in a million years.

Jack never expected an inability to read from someone so perfect. She hid it well, with poise and dignity. Hell, he'd never known another female whose name suited her more.

"Yes, you care," he said quietly. "You care a whole lot. Come here, honey."

He pulled her toward him, released her wrist and curled his arm around her shoulders. She sank against him, her forehead against his chest, and moaned his name into his shirt.

He couldn't tell if it was relief he heard—or mortification.

"This has less to do with me reading your telegram

and more to do with the fact that you're finally admitting something you've dreaded for a long while," he said.

Her head wobbled. "I hate it that you know."

"Why? Because you feel less of a person?"

"Because I *am* less of one."

He frowned. "Grace."

"You have no idea what it's like to have this…problem. It's awful."

"I suppose it would be." He wasn't going to sugarcoat the affliction. Everyone needed to read; it was a necessity, a privilege everyone should enjoy. He could only imagine the difficulties she'd lived with. "But you're an intelligent woman. Vibrant and beautiful and damned capable of doing whatever you set your mind to doing. Don't think you're not."

She shifted to rest her cheek against his shoulder and slide her arms around his waist. Taking the comfort she seemed to need. "I often feel very stupid, Jack."

"A shame you do. Because you're *not*," he stressed again.

He understood how her feelings of inferiority ran deep. Hadn't he lived with plenty inferiority of his own? Starting with the shame of growing up under Sam Ketchum's sins, then forced to wear the ugly scar he'd been given. Jack rested his chin on the top of her dark head, stroked her hair and let her talk.

"I always believed that's why my mother never wanted me," she murmured. "Because there was no hope I could get better. It was as if she didn't know what else to do but push me out of her life."

Jack declined to tell her that Bess Reilly's outlaw life wasn't fitting for a young girl anyway. Most likely Grace didn't see it that way, but Bess had done her a favor by sending her off to live a normal childhood somewhere else, with someone who loved her like she deserved.

"My grandmother did everything she could to help me learn," Grace continued. "She hired private tutors and highly educated doctors, but they just diagnosed me with word blindness and told us there was no cure."

Sympathy stirred within Jack. "Must've been hard for both of you."

"You have no idea. So Grandmother read to me constantly, doing for me what I could hardly do for myself."

"She taught you to love books."

"And so much more besides."

Though Grace didn't say it, Jack knew her work with the Ladies Literary Aid Society helped her save face by giving her a place in the Minneapolis community and a reason to hold her head high.

Unfortunately the Society and the library they wanted to build planted her right on the path toward Charles Renner. And a whole heap of trouble.

Jack drew back, and Grace's head lifted.

"I'm glad you got your word blindness off your chest, honey," he said quietly. "It was something that needed to be done. You can't keep hiding your secret away from everyone forever. Like it's some sort of terrible sin."

Distress knitted her brows. "I don't want anyone else to know, Jack. Besides you and Allie, no one does. Promise me you won't say anything."

"There's nothing to be ashamed of."

"Promise me, Jack."

Damned if he didn't sound like a hypocrite. Hadn't he turned coward, too, hiding behind the name of Hollister when he was a Ketchum, born and bred? Who was he to deny her?

"All right." Pensive, he dropped a gentle kiss to her forehead. He'd take her wishes to his grave, if that's what she wanted. "Not until you're ready."

A little sigh of relief slipped through her lips. "Thank you."

"But you're not going to keep *this* a secret from me." He tapped her nose with the telegram he still held.

"No." Looking as if she preferred the paper would up and disintegrate, she stepped away and retrieved a pair of hosiery from the bureau. "Go ahead and read it. You need to know what it says."

"I'm glad you agree," he drawled.

His glance dropped to the words scrawled in neat penmanship.

Silence her for good. LD

Jack nearly choked.

"Why the *hell* didn't you tell me sooner?" he thundered.

She whirled toward him, one delicate stocking in her hand.

"Because you occupied me with far more pleasant things to think about," she snapped back. "Would you rather I thought more of that than the love we made?"

He scowled. And some of his fury died.

But only some.

"Since Boone insisted you read the telegram, we have to assume you're the 'her' the telegram is about," he said.

"I'm afraid so." She sat on the edge of the bed with a shudder.

"It came in three days ago." His brain worked out the details. "The day you arrived in Great Falls."

"Yes."

"It's addressed to A. Thibault."

"Yes."

"And it's from Minneapolis." Wishing he could delve into her mind to pull out every man and woman she'd ever met, he pinned her with a hard gaze. "Who's LD?"

"I have no idea."

"You don't know anyone with those initials?"

"No. Not that I can recall, at least." She appealed to him, sincere and a little desperate. "But I'll keep thinking, Jack. I promise."

"It's Charles Renner."

Her throat moved with the devastation she could barely hide. "You think he's using an alias."

"Why not? Boone is."

"Yes." She glanced away to busy herself pulling a stocking onto one slender and very shapely leg. "He'd be too shrewd to sign his own name, I suppose."

"And too shrewd to use yours."

Filled with a sudden restlessness, Jack hurried to finish dressing, keenly aware of how too much time had passed, that Boone and Charles were slowly, steadily, closing in on Grace. More than ever, and soon, he had to find a way to best both men.

Then throw them into jail for a very long time.

Chapter Fifteen

Alexandre leaned back in the barber shop's leather cushioned chair, propped his feet comfortably on the matching footrest and for the first time in more months than should ever have passed, he relaxed.

He deserved the luxury of a haircut and shave. After all he'd done for the Métis people, they'd say he was entitled. No one would deny him. Not when he told them it was important that he do this for himself. For the sake of the Revolution.

He stared at the shaving mugs lined up in neat rows in front of him and let the young barber with the protruding ears prattle on while he lathered Alexandre's cheeks and neck.

Alexandre marveled at those ceramic mugs. Each one was artfully painted to reflect its owner's occupation, then personalized with his name in gold ink and fancy lettering. Cattlemen, horse breeders, telegraphers, printers, railroad conductors and engineers. Even a mortician. All of whom were valued patrons at the barber shop.

Someday, Alexandre vowed, he'd have his own shaving mug once he returned to his beloved Canada, and he entertained a variety of ways how his would be emblazoned.

Alexandre Thibault. Patriot.

Alexandre Thibault. Leader of the Métis people.

Alexandre Thibault. Revolutionist.

Or perhaps, simply…*Alexandre Thibault. Hero.*

Ah, yes. That would be the one he would choose. *Hero,* because that's what he would be, once the Revolution ended and their cause was won.

Alexandre closed his eyes and enjoyed the feel of the bristles swirling against his skin, still rough and reddened from too many hours outside, but warm, at least, from his bath. The cool sensation of the soap, the scent of castile, the feel of the straight razor sliding over his face…once he'd taken the age-old ritual for granted, but now, Alexandre gloried in all of it.

Never would he deny himself a simple haircut and shave again.

"Quite a wound you got here," the barber said, wielding the razor carefully around the tender laceration on Alexandre's forehead. "What happened?"

He'd almost forgotten how Jack Ketchum had hurled the ceramic pitcher at him back in Grace's sleeping room, that the vessel had connected with his head with such force the blood had streamed from his veins. Contempt burned a vow within Alexandre to return the painful favor. Very soon.

"I fell," Alexandre said.

"Too bad." The blade shifted direction. "Reckon it's been awhile since you've been to town," he went on cheerfully. "You're looking a little long today."

Alexandre didn't bother to open his eyes. He didn't care if the man mocked him, even in a friendly way. Alexandre knew exactly how long his hair and beard had gotten.

Too long.

What was it Grace had called him?

A savage.

Alexandre smiled to himself. He could hardly wait to see her surprise.

"I've been traveling," he said, though it was no one's business why he came to look the way he did.

"Have you now? Where from?"

Alexandre almost said Canada, but it was far more important to keep his intentions for the Revolution to himself.

"Minneapolis," he said instead.

The barber stepped to his other side, and the blade resumed its slick, efficient strokes. "Long ways from Montana. You got friends around these parts? Family?"

"I'm expecting someone to arrive by train."

"That so?"

Alexandre refused to elaborate, and the young man lapsed into a one-sided conversation about his own family, which included, apparently, a varied assortment of goldfish, all of whom Alexandre couldn't care less about.

Finally the barber wiped his razor on a towel and adjusted the chair forward. Alexandre's feet returned to the floor, liberally littered with dark hanks of his once-filthy hair.

"Well, now. You're a whole different man, aren't you?" The barber chuckled, clearly pleased with his handiwork.

"That's the idea, isn't it?"

"No one's going to recognize you, for sure."

That was the idea, too, but Alexandre didn't say so. His stare lingered over his startling new image in the mirror. A pencil-thin moustache replaced his bushy one. For the first time in untold months, he saw his cheeks, which had grown thin and sunken while he lived like an outcast, always on the move, more hungry than not.

Close-trimmed, parted on the side and swept back, his hair gleamed in the shop's lighting and filled his nostrils with the scent of the tonic combed in. He looked human again. No longer a savage, but civilized. Just like he used to be.

A gentleman ready to return to society.

Grace would find him a handsome subject in her camera lens. She would understand the importance of the photographs he needed her to take so he could send them to newspapers all over the country, along with the works he needed published. Now that he'd returned to his true identity, she was the only one who could help him succeed.

"That'll be one dollar, sir. Including the bath."

Alexandre rose from the chair, pulled back the jacket of his gray herringbone suit and withdrew a leather wallet, new like the rest of him. Plucking out a pair of bills, he handed both to the white-coated barber.

Alexandre felt no guilt that he'd taken money from the Cause; it had grown into a necessity to do so. He'd earned it, of course. A small price to pay for all he'd denied himself.

"Keep the change," he said.

The young man gaped at the bills in his palm. "Perhaps you misunderstood me, sir. This is far too much—"

"Do not insult my generosity," Alexandre snapped.

The protruding ears reddened. "No, sir. Forgive me, sir."

Alexandre pivoted toward the coatrack. The barber hastened to remove Alexandre's scarf from the hook and help him shrug into his fashionable wool overcoat.

Alexandre took great pleasure in the courtesies the man extended toward him. How long had it been since he'd been treated like this? As if he was a man of great importance? Appreciated and respected?

Too long. Much too long.

A small smile on his lips, Alexandre murmured his

thanks, donned the stylish beaver hat the barber handed him and stepped out the door. After the warmth of the barbershop, the brisk air invigorated him and refreshed his mood.

He paused on the boardwalk. A black-velvet-shrouded hearse rumbled past, and he took care to avoid the slush thrown from the wheels. He paid little mind to the lone carriage processing behind it, or to the man and woman inside. He thought only of enjoying the comforts the finest hotel in Great Falls had to offer.

Before he could head there, the shop's door opened again, and the barber rushed out. "You forgot your... things, sir."

Alexandre halted.

He eyed the bundle the man held with distaste.

"Shall I discard them for you?" the young man asked discreetly.

"Yes."

"Certainly." He turned to go back inside again.

"On second thought, no." Alexandre spoke firmly. "I'll take them, after all."

"If you're sure. It would be no trouble."

"Give my clothes to me."

Their stench sickened Alexandre. After Carl had stupidly ridden out and revealed the whereabouts of their hideout to Jack Hollister and Mick Vasco, Alexandre didn't dare return. Instead he'd been forced to spend the night in some farmer's barn, and he could still smell excrement from the pigs who had kept him warm.

Uncaring of the mud soiling his new shoes, he strode resolutely toward the nearest blacksmith shop and went inside. He ignored the sweating, beefy-armed apprentice hammering a sheet of thick metal and headed straight for the massive brick fireplace.

He threw the bundle into the roiling fire and watched his clothes burn. The fringed jacket and flat-brimmed hat. His filthy trousers and threadbare shirt and worn-out boots. All of them, gone.

Alexandre refused to be Boone ever again.

Smiling and efficient, Camille handed dinner menus to the six people Grace had come to trust most. A mixed bag of friends and lawmen who came together in a private meeting room at Margaret's Eatery to share information on the stolen money investigation. A gathering that included Mick and Allie, Paris Gibson and the private investigator he'd hired—a fortyish stockily built agent known as Kerrigan—Police Chief George Huys, and of course, the one man who had wrapped himself snugly around her heart and wouldn't let go.

Jack. Grace had never known anyone more honorable or loyal, more driven to right the wrongs committed against the innocent, no one more willing to lay down his life to enact the justice that meant so much to him.

Yes, she'd seen the cold side of him. The lawman side, fearless and hard and capable of killing, with no regrets from what had to be done.

But she'd seen the tender side of him, too—as a hot-blooded and persuasive lover. Merciful saints, the man could make a woman feel deliciously female.

She trusted him with her life.

Grace couldn't be more sure of how wrong she was in wanting to kill him. How he'd ever manage to forgive her she couldn't fathom, but Grace would spend every day of her life living with the regret from what she'd almost done.

In a mute and humble apology, she reached beneath the table and rested her hand over his denim-clad thigh. An apology she needed to express, if only by her need to touch him. Though he was engaged in conversation with George on his other side, Jack's hand moved to cover hers, as if it didn't matter what he did or who he talked with, he remained as aware of her as she was of him.

His warmth and strength revealed themselves in that simple way of touching her, and she twined her fingers with his, capturing the work-roughened feel of his skin more fully against the smoothness of her own.

His clasp tightened briefly in acknowledgment. Funny how satisfied that little gesture made her feel, and she contentedly returned her attention to her dinner menu.

She feared her rumbling stomach would announce its hunger to the far corners of Margaret's Eatery if she didn't fill it soon. Her eyes narrowed over the restaurant's meal selections, to the letters that twisted and flipped on the paper, demanding her full and undivided concentration to put them right again in her mind.

"Please accept my condolences on your brother's passing, Grace," Camille said quietly, bending near to fill her cup with steaming coffee.

Grace's finger kept her place on the menu. She'd not seen Jack's mother since yesterday morning, when they stocked the kitchen with firewood to bake their pies and Nut Cake. Was she thinking of how her husband's circumstances had been eerily similar to Carl's, that both men had been felled by her son's hand?

"Half brother," Grace murmured with a small smile. "But thank you."

"I'm sure it wasn't easy for you."

She sighed, and they exchanged a commiserating glance. "It was unfortunate, wasn't it?"

Though neither of them said so, both men suffered the same fate by the folly of their own choosing. From the crimes they committed to their rash decision to confront the lawman who was sworn to bring them in.

Instead Camille patted Grace's shoulder in sympathy.

"Yes, very unfortunate," she said. "I'll be right back to take your dinner order."

She moved on to fill Mick's and Allie's cups, too, striking Grace with the courage she showed and the example she provided, moving on with her life and leaving her husband's mistakes behind her.

Grace admired her, for it was something Grace must do as well. Carl's and her mother's decisions, right or wrong, had nothing to do with her. They never had.

"Doing okay?" Jack murmured.

His darkened eyes revealed his concern. With his Stetson propped on the corner of his chair, he wore his hair finger-combed back. Burnished-gold stubble roughened his cheeks and jaw, and Grace couldn't help remembering how that imperfectly handsome face had looked last night, shadowed in firelight while he made long, slow, incredible love to her.

"I'm fine," she said, unable to quell the attraction for him twirling through her belly.

"Been a tough morning for you." He lifted their joined hands and pressed a kiss to her knuckle, as if they were the only two people in the room. "You look tired."

She lowered her lashes and took no offense. "I'm afraid I had precious little sleep last night, thanks to you."

She kept her voice hushed, her provocative words meant for him alone. His low chuckle revealed he took full blame for the malady.

"I meant Carl, sweet," he said.

After a brief service, they'd buried him in a far, mostly neglected section of the cemetery devoted to drifters and those who died afoul of the law. Though she suspected Jack felt her half brother deserved little more than having his body rolled in canvas and dropped into a shallow grave, Grace had arranged for a simple pine casket and the dignity of being transported by hearse for his burial.

She did it as much for him as her mother, who had indeed been buried with her boots on and wrapped in that damnable canvas, without family to mourn her and only a plain wooden headboard bearing her name.

"You two done deciding what to have for dinner yet?" Mick demanded good-naturedly. "The rest of us are growing half starved waiting for you."

Grace's attention scrambled off of Jack. Cheeks warming, she sat a little taller and discovered six pairs of amused eyes over her, including Camille's, who stood waiting with them, her notepad in her hand. How long had they been watching Jack and Grace talking in near whispers, sitting as close as lovers?

All their attention left Grace flustered and her eyes unable to focus on the menu's words, let alone discern them. Fearing she'd turned the thing upside down at some point, she switched it back and forth, her panic building that she'd long since forgotten the restaurant's offerings, that she needed time, far too much time to reread the list and make up her mind.

Until Jack calmly righted the menu again and tapped his finger against a blurred line of words. "I'm having the sirloin steak. You get a potato with it and plenty of gravy."

"The macaroni and cheese is very good here, too, Grace," Allie said, her blue eyes soft with understanding.

"I say go for the meat loaf." Mick grinned.

Even the police chief smiled. "I'm a skillet hash man myself."

"There's chili, Grace, and roast beef. Don't forget Camille makes the best pies in the city if you're wanting dessert," Paris added with a wink.

"Well, my goodness," Grace said, overwhelmed.

Jack slid an arm over the back of her chair and eased back in his own, the gesture as protective as it was relaxed. "How about we order her the macaroni and cheese, Mom? I think she'll like it."

"I do, too. Good choice." Camille finished her jotting and stuffed the pad into her apron pocket. "I'll bring your dinners right out."

She hurried past the black drape cordoning the room off from the rest of the restaurant, and Grace's mortification faded. That easy, that quick, the situation was over, and not once had someone raised an eyebrow or acted in a condescending manner over her inability to comprehend the menu.

Thanks to Jack. They'd simply followed his lead and taken her slowness in stride. If anyone suspected her word blindness, they didn't show it. They didn't pity her. They didn't *mock* her.

Indeed, they'd already become engrossed in conversation with one another, leaving her filled with a bevy of emotions, not the least of them being a strong need to throw her arms around Jack and pepper his rugged face with grateful kisses.

Which she couldn't do, of course. Not here. She

settled for snuggling a little closer to him. His arm tightened and kept her there, making her wish he'd always be with her, saving her when she had trouble saving herself.

After Camille made several trips from the kitchen, Paris arranged papers around his plate. "Shall we get started? I'm afraid the news Kerrigan and I have to share on Charles Renner is disappointing in that we've been unable to secure any means of arrest."

The private investigator appeared grim. "Unfortunately, after his interrogation by the Minneapolis police, he's disappeared."

"Disappeared!" Grace exclaimed, shocked.

"Into thin air, I'm afraid."

Jack swore. A round of dismay rippled around the table.

Paris turned toward Allie. "But thanks to Jenny, we have some good news to report."

Grace recalled the petite woman of mixed ethnicity who'd been Allie's nanny since she started school. Jenny had been the one to lock Allie's trunk and the only person who could've known how the stolen money ended up inside. Suspicion pointed to her possible involvement in the embezzling scheme, but Grace always knew how Jenny loved Allie like her own daughter. It never seemed plausible the woman would want to hurt Allie in any way.

"She's signed for us a sworn statement stating

Charles gave her a sealed envelope on the day you left for Montana." Paris appeared pleased.

Allie's jaw dropped. "She did?"

"Yes. He called it a small gift for you to enjoy once you arrived west, in light of the scandal and upset you were going through with the Literary Aid Society. He made Jenny promise not to mention him or she'd spoil the surprise."

"It was a surprise, all right," Mick muttered.

Paris concurred. "So in your haste to leave Minneapolis, Jenny simply tossed the envelope into the trunk and closed it up."

"I'd only left the house for a short time to arrange for a driver," Allie said with a perplexed shake of her blond head. "Less than a half hour. He came during that time?"

"*Precisely* then, according to Jenny."

"Sounds as if he'd been watching Allie." Mick's expression revealed his disgust. "He planted the money in her trunk by way of the one woman she trusted most."

"Yes. Jenny's information is proof that Charles had stolen the library's money and tried to implicate Allie for it."

"You believe her?" Jack's gaze bounced between father and daughter.

"I do." Allie nodded gravely. "She would never betray me."

"Jenny has suffered untold guilt for her part in Allie's

troubles," Paris added. "If she hadn't dropped that envelope of money into the trunk, Allie wouldn't have been robbed."

Camille returned with the last of their dinners and slid them in front of Grace and Jack.

"I'm sorry, Jack. Forgive me for interrupting." She looked troubled. "But two men in the dining room just stopped me to ask if Grace was here. I told them she was, and they asked to see her."

Jack's gaze sharpened. "Who are they?"

"I don't know. I've never seen them before, but they're fashionable and very courteous." Camille's glance slid toward the drape, carefully closed as if she tried to protect Grace in that small way. "Something about them didn't feel right, though. There's a certain, well, arrogance about them."

Jack slanted the police chief a look. "Grace is new in town. She doesn't know anybody, arrogant or otherwise."

As if a sudden thought dawned, he swung his glance toward her.

"Except Boone," they said together.

"It's not Boone." Camille shook her head.

"I don't want her talking to them, whoever they are." Jack was solemn serious.

His mother hesitated. "I told them she's not feeling well, so they left. No questions asked."

Jack's brow arched in surprise. "That easy?"

"Yes." She nodded quickly.

"Smart thinking."

"Was it?" She turned her apologetic glance toward Grace. "I hope I wasn't too presumptuous."

"You weren't." The police chief shook his head. "Until we know what's afoot, it's too dangerous to expose Grace to someone she's not expecting. If they were acquaintances of hers, they would've sent word of their arrival."

The truth in the lawman's logic chilled her. Grace couldn't fathom who the two men might be. She had no family in this part of the country, and all her friends lived hundreds of miles away in Minnesota.

No one she knew would come to Montana to see her.

No one she trusted.

She was safe, Grace told herself. Except for Paris and Allie, Jack and the others were armed. If the two strangers had even the most remote of illicit intentions, they were badly outnumbered by the men in this room.

Still, the way Jack diverted his glance into a slow perusal around the perimeter of the private dining area unnerved her. The backup plan he formulated in his mind, she knew. A means of escape if they must.

She had no idea how they'd manage it. Their quarters contained no door and only a small window. Grace doubted she could climb through the narrow opening under the best of circumstances, let alone Jack. The only way out remained through the back of the kitchen and the front of the restaurant.

Either way, they were sitting ducks.

As if he'd come to the same conclusion, Jack swung a hard glance toward his mother. "Didn't happen to get their names, did you?"

"Sorry, no. I didn't ask, and they didn't offer. They just expressed concern for Grace and said they'd be in contact with her later."

"Damn." Jack didn't look pleased.

"They were very nice." Camille sighed. "In fact, now I'm thinking I shouldn't have been so suspicious. It seems unfair to them."

"And maybe they have an ulterior motive. Grace hasn't exactly had an easy time of it since she got here." Jack stabbed his sizzling steak with his fork, as if it contained all his frustrations. "We have to be careful. Each one of us. Until that money is found and the guilty parties are in custody, we can't trust anyone."

"For now, at least, it seems the threat has passed. Let's continue on with our meeting, shall we?" Paris returned to his notes with the focus of a man accustomed to seeing his commitments through. "The sooner we can finish, the sooner we can return to solving the case. I'm confident the information we've gleaned on Charles will help us accomplish that."

"I'll be right back with more coffee for all of you." Camille pivoted toward the black drape.

But at the sound erupting on the other side, she froze.

Everyone's heads swung toward the drape, too.

Rumbles from the dinner patrons, Grace realized with growing alarm. An odd and unexpected rise of noise that warned of something amiss. Something none of them could see, but knew shouldn't be happening.

Something terribly wrong.

Camille dashed past the partition. Jack bolted to his feet with an abruptness that clattered his chair, but before Grace could follow, before any of them could, his mother screamed and toppled back into the room with a violence that nearly ripped the drape from its rod, shoved to the floor by the two men forcing their way inside.

Neckerchiefs covered their faces, goggles shielded their eyes, their tall, well-dressed bodies demonized by the angry swirls of smoke shrouding them from the bombs they gripped in their fists. One after another, they hurled the bombs into the room, filling the air with an acrid sting, coloring the place grayish-white.

Chairs crashed to the floor. Savage oaths and terrified screams. Jack went for his gun. Mick, too, Kerrigan and George, but by some unspoken command, no one fired, no one dared. Not in air too thick, too stinging, the danger of one of them being accidentally hit too great....

"Get down, get down!" Jack choked out, but Grace already felt herself crumpling, her body racked by coughing. She squeezed her eyes against the terrible sting. She couldn't breathe, couldn't move, couldn't think. She needed air. Sweet, fresh air...

Grunts and oaths penetrated the deep fog that surrounded her. Noise, so much noise and confusion. Men yelling, women screaming, furniture crashing, glass shattering.

Strong arms banded around her, lifting her high above the floor. She clung to the arms, to the lean body cradling her against his chest, saving her, taking her away from the awful smoke.

Something soft covered her face; her nose and her lungs instantly reacted, sucking inward.

Sucking her into a black abyss.

Chapter Sixteen

"She's coming to."

Grace clawed through the oblivion and grasped onto the shredded reality of a voice. Someone male, someone close. Her eyes cracked open. Her brain swam to comprehend her surroundings.

A tiny shack. Squalid and cold. A lone kerosene lamp illuminated the cobwebs clinging to the rafters. A dirty blanket covered her, and she lay on a hard, narrow cot. Blurred shapes of two men stood over her, watching her, and oh, God!

She scrambled to sit up, flinging aside the foul covering as if it was reeking meat. Assailed with dizziness, she grabbed the edge of the cot.

"Careful." One of the men reached out a hand, as if sure she'd fall. "You need a little more time."

She stared at him in the lantern's light. Darkly

handsome, with a thin moustache, neatly trimmed hair. Black eyes and one slightly angled eyetooth...

"What I need is out of here." Her voice didn't sound like her own, but raspy and desperate. "Damn you, Boone. Get me out of here!"

"Alexandre." The word quivered with warning. "Never call me Boone again."

Grace saw her mistake and learned from it. "Of course." She nodded carefully, knowing she had to play the game. "Forgive me."

He straightened to his full height. In his gray herring-bone suit, he appeared a man of influence. Well-bred and proud. "Are you strong enough yet? Our work must begin."

She didn't move. "Where are we? Where's Jack?"

"Forget Jack." The second man spoke. "He is of no use to you now."

Her stare swiveled. Recognition slammed into her belly, stealing her breath. A man so handsome, so cunning and capable of betrayal, her heart squeezed with instant hate.

"Hello, Charles." Grace stood on legs barely steady. "How strange it must feel for you to be hiding here in the cold and filth when you're accustomed to...finer pleasures."

"It will not be forever."

"Yet for Alexandre, who has lived no better than a savage, it did seem that way. Forever." Her glance touched on the other man. She understood the fragile threads that kept her tethered to Boone. She feigned her compassion. "Didn't it, Alexandre?"

A muscle in his lean cheek leapt. "Yes."

"It had to be done," Charles snapped coldly.

"Of course. By someone other than yourself." She reined in her contempt and regarded him. "Your name isn't really Charles Renner, is it?"

He hesitated, the barest of moments. "No."

"Then what shall I call you?"

"Charles, as you always have. It is who I am to you."

"I want to know the truth."

Because he'd lied to her so often, for so long, it was imperative to Grace to know. To be less of a fool.

"It won't hurt to tell her," Alexandre said, a hint of impatience in his voice. "She sympathizes with us."

Words to deny him sprang fast on her tongue. Sympathize? Hardly. Yet she didn't dare speak her denial, not when she needed Boone as her ally, needed to retain his trust.

"She has not earned the truth," Charles told him.

"Oh?" Grace crossed her arms against the cabin's chill. Or maybe it was this frigid side of Charles that left her cold. "Have I not acted as a friend to you from the time we were introduced? I've been nothing short of sincere in all of my dealings with you, as had my grandmother, Allethaire and everyone else in the Society."

"Then you served your purpose for me, did you not?"

"As your pawn for stealing the funds you helped us raise?" she shot back.

"I worked as hard as you did for that money, Grace," he snarled. "Harder, in fact."

"And that gives you the right to—to just take it in an elaborate scheme—"

"You will never be able to prove anything." He appeared so calm, Grace shivered. "I have all your grandmother's records."

She went still. The records from her satchel? The ones she'd kept in the hatbox so she could *incriminate* him?

"Where are they?" She needed to see the red-ribboned hatbox for herself, to know he was telling the truth. Because she was afraid he was, and she didn't want to believe him. She prayed he was just lying again, as skillfully as he'd always lied.

"Did you think you were so clever, Grace?" He appeared amused. "Hiding them in a satchel where even a hapless mouse could find them?"

She battled panic. "Those papers belong to the Society. Not to you or to me. You have to give them back, Charles, or the library project will surely fail. You know what a loss that would be. You know!"

He swung toward Alexandre. "Let us hurry. It will be dark soon."

With a quick nod, Alexandre stepped aside, toward a crudely built table, and there laid the hatbox, looking woefully feminine and out of place in the squalor. Forgotten, almost, begging for Grace to take it back.

She'd have to find a way, but for now, sitting next to the hatbox, a brown bottle plainly labeled Ammonium Nitrate and the small pile of rolled up newspapers, tied in string, reminded her of the violence these two men were capable of.

The smoke bombs were only the beginning.

Her pulse pounded in worry for all she'd left behind. Had anyone been hurt? Jack? Allie or Mick or the others?

Grace trembled from knowing if they were, it would be her fault. Everything was her fault. The violence, the terror—if she could only read like any other educated adult, if she hadn't come to Great Falls to seek Allie's help in deciphering her grandmother's records pertaining to the Ladies Literary Aid Society, then none of this would be happening.

Worse, it was far from over. Charles and Boone had gone to a great deal of trouble to bring her out here to this dilapidated shack. They believed she was worth the risk. That she was of some benefit to them.

She couldn't fathom why. Or how.

"Come, Grace." From seemingly out of nowhere, Boone produced her camera. Her prized Kodak, stolen out of her satchel, too.

He thrust it at her, gripped her elbow and pulled her toward the door. "The light won't last much longer."

"Remember she has no coat, Alexandre. She cannot

work for you half-frozen." Charles plucked the musty blanket off the cot. "Wrap her in this."

"What is it I am to do, Alexandre?" she asked, ignoring Charles and the careless way he draped the dirty blanket over her shoulders.

"Take my picture, Grace." With an eagerness that attested to the vanity he'd too long kept suppressed, Boone half pushed her out the door and past two horses, tethered at a post. "As many as I want."

"You want me to photograph you?" Outside, her steps faltered. She blinked up at him, partly from the sharp cold, partly from shock. "Whatever for?"

The words were no sooner out of her mouth than she realized her mistake. She remembered the game she had to play, the trust she needed to keep, and she hastened to reclaim her place in Boone's fanatical mind.

"Oh, of course." Instantly she stopped fighting him. "I understand now. How could I have forgotten?" She managed an acknowledging nod. "For...the Revolution."

His lips curved with approval beneath the thin moustache. "What else, my love?" He wore no coat himself, but it didn't seem to matter. "Many times, I've thought of how best to present myself to this country and my own. I know now, and you will help me."

The soles of Grace's button oxford shoes slipped over the crusty, uneven snow. Now that she was outside, she must get her bearings and discern her location, because once these pictures were taken, Charles and Boone would flee. Boone would take her with him, driven by the infatuation he felt for her and the misguided belief that she'd be a perfect tool with which to help him win his Revolution.

Besides, she knew too much.

A mountain stream sparkled beneath the setting sun and flowed beyond an outcropping of rock. Alongside, a line of trees, and in the distance, Great Falls sprawled... and she knew, then, where she was. Where she'd been just yesterday with Allie. Where Carl and Boone had been hiding out from the law, and where Carl had been killed.

That Boone dared to return with Charles instilled Grace with renewed urgency. She had to find a way to escape and soon. Jack would know of this place. Mick, too, but if they didn't come, if something had happened to them back at Margaret's Eatery, then she'd have no one to turn to for help.

Except herself.

"Here, Grace. This is where I shall stand." Boone released her elbow and strode toward a large rock, jutting from the banks of the stream. In his zeal for the perfect pose, he propped his foot on top, rested his hand on his thigh and angled his head toward the north. "We're not far from Canada, and this view reminds me of the beauty, the wildness of my country."

The snowcapped Bear Tooth Mountains loomed in the distance. Douglas firs, long-needled pines and various species of spruce grew along the foothills. Puffs of clouds decorated the blue-gray sky, and Grace conceded the backdrop was indeed fitting for a man of Boone's compulsion.

Yet she thought more of escape. Now, in the coming moments, while Boone was distracted and preening. Pretending interest in their surroundings, she gauged the plausibility of running away, but as soon as she spied Charles watching them at the cabin's door, a revolver leveled in her direction, she abandoned the idea.

He'd shoot her dead if she tried.

Besides, she had no coat, no horse…

"My profile first, Grace. It's appropriate, don't you think?" Boone asked.

Grace had little recourse but to follow along. The photographs were harmless, she supposed, something she could do to feed his fantasy and keep her outside, in easy view in case Jack happened to be riding this way.…

"Quite appropriate, yes." She carefully bettered her grasp over the black box. She found him in the camera's lens, cocked the shutter and turned the key to advance the film. "Don't move, Alexandre." She pressed the trigger. "There."

Obviously pleased and enjoying himself, he struck one pose after another, keeping Grace busy with snapping shots of him until she was almost out of film, until her fingers grew too numb to work the camera.

"Enough, Alexandre." Charles called out. "You have more than enough photographs. Bring Grace back inside."

His aquiline nose reddened from the cold, Boone acknowledged the command and once again took her elbow, assisting her across the snow.

"When can you have them ready?" he asked, his breath billowing.

"The photographs?" she asked.

"Yes, yes. How do you get them out of the box?"

She hesitated. "I can't."

He nudged her inside the shadowed cabin and shoved the door closed. He appeared taken aback. "What do you mean you can't?"

"I have no experience in developing the film, Alexandre."

Charles gestured for her to sit in a chair placed at the table. Grace longed for the heat from a roaring fire, but the block was empty, she knew, for the smoke that would curl from the chimney, giving them away. She had to settle for clutching the dirty blanket closer about her shivering shoulders.

"Then how am I to get my photographs?" Boone demanded.

"I must return the camera to the company who manufactured it." She kept her voice even. Patient. And understood how her explanation would impair the expediency of his plan. "They are the ones who will print them. Then they will send the photographs back to me."

"Unthinkable," Charles said.

Boone ignored him. He stepped closer to Grace. "How long will it take?"

"I *said* it is unthinkable, Alexandre," Charles thundered. "It is too simple for someone to recognize you and trace you back to Grace. And we cannot reveal her whereabouts. So forget the photographs."

"I will not forget them." Fury darkened Boone's expression.

Charles snatched a coil of rope off the table. "You must."

"Maybe another photographer can get them out of the camera." He swung back toward her. "Can he?"

"I don't know." Grace spoke honestly. "Maybe."

Charles emitted a disgusted curse. "Now your photographs have become a foolish waste of time. We cannot shop around for someone with the ability to make the pictures."

"Foolish?" Boone echoed. "Waste of time?"

"There are far more important things you can do for the sake of the Cause." Charles stepped around the table, toward Grace, the coil of rope in his hand.

"And how many photographs have *you* had taken, Louis David?" he demanded sharply. "With your friends and the beautiful women who have surrounded you all these months, while you recline in comfort?"

"I dedicate myself to the Cause as much as you, Alexandre." Charles's nostrils flared from the anger he could barely hold in check. "My methods are just as effective as yours." He paused with an arrogant tilt of his brow. "More, in fact."

"I'll find another way to get my photographs out of the Kodak box." Boone fairly shook from the resolve.

Grace eyed the rope Charles held with growing trepidation. Clearly, the men had no intention of staying in the cabin. No fire, no food and too much risk prevented it.

But it was their intentions for *her* that lifted the fine hairs on the back of her neck. An ugly premonition growing uglier with every step Charles took toward her....

She bolted out of the chair to the door, but too quick, Boone grabbed her and pushed her back into the seat, and before she could even think it, Charles looped the rope again and again around her flailing body, binding her to the back of the chair so tightly she could hardly breathe, let alone scream.

"Damn you, damn you both!" She kicked out at Charles, then at Alexandre, narrowly missing both sets of shins. "How dare you!"

Alexandre's dark eyes darted from Charles to Grace and back at Charles.

"What is the meaning of this?" he demanded in a voice so low, so lethal, Grace realized he'd not known what his accomplice had intended.

"We have no further use for her."

"She is mine now, Louis David. Mine."

"She is a hindrance!" Charles swung toward his coat and shoved his arms into the sleeves. "We must get rid of her. She will only slow us down." He jerked toward the cabin's only window. "Look outside. Do you not see how late it is? How time is working against us?"

"This is not the plan we agreed upon."

"The plan must change."

"Alexandre." Grace tried one more time to appeal to the man's vulnerability, the hurting part of him that nurtured his infatuation with her. "Alexandre, please. The ropes are hurting me. Please untie me."

"Shut up, Grace." Charles grabbed the lantern off the shelf.

"I don't care about the money anymore." Grace ignored Charles and leaned toward Alexandre, as far as the bindings allowed. "I know now why you stole it, and I can help you. You know I can."

"Do not listen to her. Put your coat on." Charles tossed Boone the garment one-handed. "We must leave. Now."

Alexandre caught the coat, but he didn't put it on. "You understand why my people are oppressed, don't you, Grace?"

"Yes." More than ever, Grace wished that Jack was here. She'd fallen headfirst into the hole she was digging for herself, so deep she feared she couldn't get out. "Yes, you know I do."

"You'll try to help me save them? To organize the government they need to survive?"

"Yes!"

"No-o! She is lying, Alexandre! Stop listening to

her!" Enraged, Charles slammed the lantern against the wall.

The fuel splattered, and the flames roared outward, latching onto the cabin's side and rafters and refusing to let go, ravenous for the old wooden logs that would feed its frenzy.

Grace screamed.

Boone yelled in fury.

Suddenly the window's glass shattered. The nose of a rifle jammed inward, and Mick's face appeared through the opening. In the next moment, the cabin's door flew open, so fast, so hard, it rocked on its hinges, and there stood Jack, tall and ruthless with a gun in each hand....

Boone whipped toward him with his weapon, and Jack coldly fired. Blood spurted across the front of the gray herringbone suit. Boone screamed and spun to his knees, losing his grip on the rifle.

"Do not shoot!" Charles crouched against the flames and half crawled toward the door. "Please, please, do not shoot!"

"Get out." Jack grabbed him by his coat and shoved him to George Huys, waiting outside to catch him.

Mick dashed in. "You hit, Jack?"

"No, Boone is. Help me get him out of here."

Combining their muscle, they lifted him from the floor. Mick took his weight and rushed him out of the blazing cabin.

The flames grew hotter, their fiery arms reached

closer, nearly singeing Grace with their ferocious bite. She strained against the ropes and screamed Jack's name.

And then, he was there.

Chapter Seventeen

The roar of the fire poured pure, unadulterated terror into Jack's blood. Grace was alive, and she didn't look hurt, but seeing her trussed up, left to burn, to die, had him shaking so hard he could barely undo the ropes. With Grace's frantic help, he managed it.

He hauled her out of the chair with both hands. "Let's get out of here!"

But she pushed against him. "My hatbox, Jack!"

She broke from his grasp and lunged toward the burning table. He could barely discern the shape of the thing through the thickening smoke, but she seemed to know right where it was and grabbed it fast, whirling back toward him. He hooked his arm around her shoulders and dragged her out of the cabin, far enough away that the fire and smoke couldn't touch them anymore.

Grace didn't need to explain how that damn box

ended up on the table, in this squalid hideout, all the way out here on the mountain. Charles and Boone had known the papers inside would be evidence against them, and they'd set out to destroy every piece. Right along with Grace. Shutting her up. For good.

They'd almost succeeded.

She dragged in air, coughed and coughed again. Jack opened his coat and held her hard against him, warming her, holding her until she quieted and sank against his chest.

He closed his eyes and let the fear of losing her seep out of him. He pressed his scarred cheek into her hair.

"I love you, Grace. I love you," he said.

Her head lifted with a tiny gasp, and her wide gaze met his. She seemed about to say something until footsteps crunched in the snow.

"Excuse me, Jack." The police chief looked grim, but his expression revealed his concern, too. "Doing all right, young lady?" he asked.

She stood a little taller and kept one arm clutched around the scorched hatbox, the other around Jack's waist. "Much better than I was a few minutes ago, thank you."

"We spied you out here with him, you know. Taking pictures by the stream. Jack had a hunch Boone or Alexandre or whatever the hell he calls himself would come back to his old stomping grounds."

"It was the safest and farthest place he could take her," Jack said, glad his instincts hadn't failed him.

"After smoking us out of the restaurant, he had to disappear in a hurry. Grace didn't even have a coat."

"Well, they're not going to disappear now." The lawman nodded in somber satisfaction. "We've got 'em where we want 'em."

He turned toward the tree line, and Jack spied Charles sitting on a bed of fallen ponderosa pine needles, handcuffed to the tree's trunk with his knees pulled up and his head hanging down. Tethered with him, the horses that would've helped him escape.

"How sad that he brought this all on himself," Grace said. "Without a care to the scores of people he hurt back in Minneapolis."

"He's paying the price for it." George seemed far less affected. "That one, though, isn't going to make it." He indicated Boone, lying in crimson-stained snow.

Mick stood over him, his rifle loose in his hand, guarding him against any moves he wasn't likely to make.

"He needs a doctor," she said quietly.

"Won't do him any good," George said. "He's already knocking on Hell's door, I'm afraid."

Jack shrugged out of his coat and draped it over Grace's shoulders. He strode toward the outlaw. For a moment, he stood over him, too, like Mick, looking down at the man who had too long lived on the wrong side of the law.

Boone could've been Sam Ketchum laying there, shot

half-dead from Jack's gun. The similarities, the irony, were too strong to ignore.

I gotta know...who set me up. Find him for me, y'hear? Will you do that...for your ol' man, Jack?

Knowing he had, finally, Jack hunkered down and gently rolled Boone toward him. Pale, ashen, his breathing rattled, Boone didn't have much time left.

But still, Jack had to hear it.

"It was you that night, wasn't it?" he asked. "Down in New Mexico."

Glazed with pain, the black eyes fluttered over him. "You always thought you were better than him...didn't you?"

"Not better." Far from it. Still, the words stung. Even now. Even from Boone. "We just made different mistakes, that's all."

"Knew...you'd go after him. Jus' like I told you to."

"It had to be done."

And if Jack hadn't, if Boone had never tracked him down in the Sierra Grande Mountains to reveal the Ketchum gang's hideout, where would they all be now? Who would have died? Who'd still be alive?

Jack would give anything to change that night.

But then, if not for Boone and his greed, Jack would never have met Grace.

Setting the hatbox aside, out of reach, she knelt beside him, her skirts a vibrant blue against the crystalline snow. "When you betrayed Sam Ketchum, Alexandre, you betrayed my mother, too."

Boone grimaced, as if on a wave of pain. Physical or otherwise, Jack couldn't be sure. "She was...nothing like you."

"Unfortunately it doesn't matter anymore." Grace leaned forward, and his dark gaze clung to her. As if her presence helped him breathe. To survive a little while longer. "You have a chance to redeem yourself before it's too late."

"Not...too late."

"Oh, but it is." She bit her lip, as if to rein in her desperation. "Tell us where you hid the Society's money. Please, Alexandre."

He choked out a bitter laugh. "You are consumed by it, my love."

"Just as you are."

"For my...people."

"It was never theirs. It wasn't."

His black eyes closed, then opened again. He coughed, grimaced and eased back. A trickle of blood slid out the corner of his mouth.

"No one...knows where I hid it." He halted, dragged in air. "Not even Louis...David."

"Alexandre, please. While you still can, tell me," Grace pleaded.

Gurgling sounds slid from the outlaw's throat. His eyes rolled back. He didn't move, didn't breathe, for too long, and Jack knew then, he was gone.

"We've lost him, honey," he said, grimly.

She pressed her fingers to her mouth in dismay.

Mick shook out a blanket and covered him. "I'm sorry, Grace. He didn't have a thing to lose in telling you where that money was. Wasn't fair to you."

She sighed, so damned dejected Jack's heart hurt for her.

"Did he pass on?" George asked, joining them.

"He did." Jack stuck a thumb in his hip pocket and pondered their chances of finding the missing loot. Ever.

"Damned shame, for sure." The police chief gestured to Mick. "Give me a hand, will you?"

"Sure thing."

Jack stepped aside, taking Grace with him. She didn't need to see the macabre nature of their work, the indignity of a man strapped to his horse with his toes pointing down.

"Hold me, Jack," Grace said.

She slipped out of his coat, and he put it on again, then pulled her against him; she slid her arms around to his back, helping herself to his warmth, and laid her head on his chest. He pulled the edges of his coat as snugly around her as he could.

"The money could be anywhere in the territory," she said, sounding sad. Frustrated.

"There's ways to track it down, Grace." He rested his chin on the top of her ebony head. For her sake, he tried to stay positive, to give her hope. "The investigation is far from over. We're learning more about those two all the time." He recalled the information Paris had wanted to share with them about Charles Renner over dinner. Before they'd been attacked with the smoke bombs. "We'll track down every lead, clear into Canada if we have to."

She sighed again. "It's all so bizarre. Just yesterday, it was as if Boone lived in the dregs of the earth."

As far as Jack knew, Boone had been just like that. The dregs of the earth. For years. From the time he'd been a part of the Ketchum gang.

"Today, he looked as rich as anyone could be," Grace finished.

Jack frowned. Wouldn't have been cheap for a man to transform himself like that. From his head to his toes. From the inside out.

"Maybe he dipped into the till," he mused.

Her head lifted in surprise. "Do you think so?"

"The money had to come from somewhere."

"Yes." She drew back. "Somewhere close."

"He wouldn't carry it with him, and he didn't keep it in the hideout. Leastways, he didn't act like it when the fire started."

"No." Deep in thought, she nibbled on her lip.

"He wouldn't have put it in an account somewhere, either." Jack's thoughts came, rapid-fire. "Too risky. And there's been no evidence of an accomplice around town, except for Carl."

Jack knew for sure the kid didn't have a dime on him when he died. Besides, if Boone had any sense at all—

and Jack knew he did—Boone wouldn't have trusted Carl as far as he could spit.

"Maybe he buried it somewhere," Grace said.

"Would've been the safest thing," Jack concurred.

"Somewhere out of the way, but not too hard to find."

"So he could get to it quick, if he had to."

His mind worked over an image he'd all but forgotten until now. A memory from yesterday afternoon, when Boone had hunkered along the stream, doing something Jack couldn't see....

At the time, he'd wondered about it. But his concern had been focused more on Grace, boldly off her horse and talking to the outlaw with his rifle trained right over her. Then Carl came riding out, all hell had broken loose and Jack had forgotten about it.

Until now.

Suddenly Grace pushed away from him with a loud gasp. "Yesterday afternoon, Boone was—"

"I know," Jack said, taking her hand.

"I think he buried it—"

"In the water." He started to run.

She lifted her skirts and ran with him, her steps light and graceful over the snow. "Oh, Jack, I know right where he was."

Adrenaline coursed through his veins. They sprinted toward the crisp, glittering stream and rounded the outcropping of rock, past the spot where Carl had dropped from his horse and died, and headed right to the water's edge.

Automatically Jack shrugged out of his coat, tossing it over Grace's shoulders for the second time in a matter of minutes, but she didn't seem to notice. She stared at the prints in the snow, same as he did. Jack found the spot where Boone had knelt, even the one where his rifle had been, set aside while he worked.

And there, wrapped around a smooth, glistening rock, so incongruous no one would've seen it, not in a million years, was one end of a narrow strip of rawhide, extending down into the water, where the other end held its treasure in place.

"Merciful saints," Grace breathed. "There it is."

Jack hunkered down and tugged on the rawhide. The weight gave, and he lifted a parcel snugly encased in india rubber out of the water. "Isn't that about the prettiest thing you've ever seen, honey?"

She squealed. "Open it, Jack. Hurry! We have to be sure."

But Jack was. As sure as flowers in May.

He made short work of untying the rawhide and opening the rubber. A tattered envelope appeared, as tattered as it had been that fateful day when Allie tore it open, discovering the crime planted against her while she traveled on the St. Paul, Minneapolis & Manitoba Railway train, headed to Great Falls.

Moments later, an outlaw named Reggie had plucked the envelope bulging with cash right out of her hands. Boone and Carl had been with him, and all three men escaped with the loot, leaving her behind to deal with the consequences.

Hell of an ordeal they'd put Allie and Grace through.

But now, today, the money would be returned to the Ladies Literary Aid Society, where it belonged.

"Is it all there, Jack?" Grace asked, leaning into him while her fingers riffled through the cash.

"Seems so." A corner of his mouth lifted. "Minus the cost of a good haircut and an even better suit."

George and Mick hustled toward them.

"Everything okay over here?" Mick asked.

The police chief almost slipped and fell in his haste. "We heard a ruckus."

Jack pulled Grace against him. "A happy ruckus, George. And that's a promise."

A carriage rumbled up the mountain. Paris sat in the driver's seat with Allie next to him. Along with the private investigator, Kerrigan, one of George's deputies escorted them up.

Grace squealed again, jumped up and down and waved her arms.

"We found the money, Allie. We found it!" she shouted.

"You did?" Allie shouted back. She half stood in her surprise. "Oh, Grace, truly?"

"Yes, yes!"

Allie jumped out of the rig before her father braked to a full stop. Grace ran toward her, and the two women hugged and danced, leaving the rest of them grinning at their glee.

"A fine piece of investigative work you did, Jack." George shook his head in amazement. "You solved the case for us."

"Yeah, well." His gaze lingered over Grace. He soaked in the sight of her happiness and took pleasure in knowing he had a part in it. "I had help."

"Not much, and you know it." He extended his hand, and Jack clasped it in his own. "I appreciate everything you did. Anytime you want a job, let me know. I'll have one waiting for you." He thumped Jack on the shoulder. "You're a fine lawman. I'd be proud to have you on the force."

Heady words, for sure, and they took root deep in Jack's chest, swelling his heart with pride. He figured he'd come full circle since his father's death. Sam Ketchum wouldn't know how Jack had fallen into punishing grief, but it was Sam's need to avenge his betrayer that pulled Jack up and out of the guilt by his bootstraps.

The old man had done him a favor. He'd forced Jack to realize his dream had never died.

Being a lawman was who he was meant to be.

"Thanks, George," he said. "Means a lot that you think so." They clasped hands. "We'll talk soon."

Paris approached. "It's true, then. The two hooligans responsible for the embezzling scheme have been caught?"

Jack nodded. "For good."

"Charles Renner was an alias, you know. Just like Boone was for Alexandre Thibault."

"I figured as much."

"Kerrigan dug up information that proved Louis David Riel is Renner's real name. He's a political revolutionist who's been working to overthrow the Canadian government in favor of his own people."

Jack recalled all Boone had claimed. "The Métis people."

"That's right. There are some who call Riel a fanatic. Others call him a prophet. Still others claim he's a lunatic who needs to be committed to an asylum." Paris grunted, as if the man was more than he could comprehend. "Regardless, he'll be going back to Canada. Likely tried for treason."

Jack could only shake his head at the shame of it all.

Paris regarded him with a fatherly expression. A wise one, too. "Go on, take Grace back to Lindell's." He winked. "Warm her up. It's cold as a witch's tits out here."

In spite of himself, Jack chuckled. "I like the way you think, Paris."

He turned and headed across the snow to do just that.

Later that night, much later, Jack couldn't sleep.

A warm fire crackled in the block, filling Grace's room with golden light. The incessant ticking of the bedside clock served as a constant reminder of how fast time could speed by when a man wanted it to stop.

He wished the night would never end so he could keep on holding Grace in his arms, both of them naked and curled around one another like puppies in a basket. If Jack could find a way to keep the sun from rising again, he would. If he never had to leave this room, this bed, he wouldn't.

The hell of it was…none of those things would ever happen, and that meant he couldn't stop Grace from leaving him.

And she would, he knew. She had to. She had responsibilities back in Minneapolis, her commitment to the community and the Ladies Literary Aid Society. As president, she had to carry on her grandmother's work and see the library done, once and for all.

Besides, Grace wasn't cut out for life in Montana's rough, barely settled territory. She wasn't near used to it. Bess Reilly saw to it that her daughter was raised in a gentler way, surrounded by society's rich and the privileges that came with it.

Jack held Grace a little tighter and thought of how he was as ill-suited to big-city life as she was to the one here. After his father's death, Montana had been Jack's salvation. The people of Great Falls, Mick and Trey and the rest of the outfit at the Wells Cattle Company… they'd helped him heal. To start over in anonymity.

He owed it to them all to stay and give back some of what they'd given him. He had to do what he could to police the lawless and keep the citizens safe, to help the territory settle and thrive.

Would Grace understand how he could do nothing less?

Or would she even care what he did? Their time together had been so damned short. No courtship, no wooing, no playing by society rules…and yet their coupling *seemed* like he meant something to her. From the moment they'd stepped into this room and fallen together on the bed, Grace was a fireball of passion and tenderness, wildly giving and taking until she damn near wore him out from their loving.

How would he ever let her go?

A quivery little sigh scooted over his chest, and surprised, he drew back a little to see her.

"I thought you were sleeping," he murmured, sliding his fingers through her hair, brushing the strands off her temple.

"I can't."

"Me, neither." He pressed a kiss to her dark head and debated the merits of making love to her again. To help them both forget the time and how fast it marched them through the night.

"Jack. I have something to tell you."

He sensed her hesitation, her dread, and his stomach clenched.

"I suspect you do," he said.

She took a breath, let it out again. He imagined how

hard it was for her to say what she was about to say. What he knew was coming.

"I'm taking the morning train back to Minneapolis," she blurted.

"I expected you would."

But damn, it cut right through him to hear her say it. He'd braced for it, known it, but still it hurt like a bitch.

Now, it was real.

"I must continue my grandmother's work. You know I must, don't you?"

"I do."

"The library means so much to me. Providing books, the opportunity to read—oh, the cultural benefits are enormous, and thousands of people will benefit. Thousands, Jack."

"You don't have to convince me, honey. I already understand."

"There are untold details to tend to. After the scandal of Charles's embezzling, the press will have to be dealt with. Accountants and bankers, and who knows what else. It'll be like starting all over again."

"You'll have your work cut out for you, for sure."

"The Ladies will *expect* me to be there, leading them through this endeavor."

"You can't let them down, can you?

A moment passed.

"Jack." She rose up on her elbow. The sheet slipped, revealing one delectably round breast. With blue eyes wide and voluminous, she stared at him. Her lower lip quivered. "Don't you want me to stay?"

He blinked. His brain turned somersaults to comprehend the switch to her logic.

"Stay?" he rumbled. *"Stay?"*

On a growl of pain and frustration, he flipped her over to her back with an abruptness that wobbled the mattress. He straddled her, glaring down at her with a ferocity he couldn't curtail.

"You think it's not tearing me up inside, listening to you detail how your life is going to be halfway across the country?" he demanded. "A life that will never include me?"

"But it could, Jack. Come with me tomorrow, and—"

"No."

She sucked in a breath. "Why?"

"I can't." He thought anew of his obligations right here in Great Falls, the debt he owed to the townspeople, and his jaw tightened.

"You can't? Or won't?" There that full lip went, getting all quivery again.

"Call it what you want, honey, but I'm not going. It would likely destroy us both."

And Jack couldn't risk losing what they had, every raw and vulnerable *perfect* moment of it.

"Minneapolis has a fine police force, Jack. They'd be *proud* to have a lawman like you in their ranks."

An image of George Huys slipped into his mind.

Not once had it mattered to the man that Jack was an outlaw's son. At the outset, from the moment Jack had introduced himself, the police chief had trusted him for who he was, for the reputation Jack had earned despite the blemish of his father's crimes.

Would Minneapolis be so forgiving?

Somehow, Jack didn't think so.

"I'm in love with you, Grace. You're the most perfect woman I've had the pleasure of knowing, but I can't go with you. And I can't ask you to stay here in the territory."

"But—"

"Not until you're ready." Maybe she never would be, but it was a chance he had to take. "We'll both know when the time is right."

He eased down over her, ever so slowly, belly to belly, thigh to thigh, the fire to have her again, to show her how much he hated losing her from his life, building again in his groin.

"Jack." Her eyes, always a perfect shade of blue, filled with moisture.

He lowered his head, licked her neck, inhaled the fragrance of her skin.

"When you're ready, Grace honey, you'll know where to find me," he murmured.

He could only hope she would. Be ready. If she never was, if she couldn't love him…well, it would rank right up there with one of the worst times of his life, and he wasn't going to think of it.

Not when he wanted to think of things far more pleasurable.

A trail of tears streamed down her cheek, and he kissed them away, tenderly, lovingly. She curled her arms around his neck, held him close and breathed his name.

"Yes," she whispered. "Yes, I will."

She gave him hope, fragile and tenuous and maybe nothing would come of it, but he clung to the hope just the same. Time took on new meaning, gave him one last chance to show her just how much he was going to miss her.

Which he did.

Until the night was gone.

Epilogue

Spring

Preparations for Allie and Mick's wedding were in full swing at the Wells Cattle Company, a two-day event that included invitations to several hundred people from throughout the territory, surrounding states and beyond. Paris spared no expense for the most important occasion in his only daughter's life, and the wedding promised to be the social event of the year.

Which only worried Grace all the more.

Not that she would've missed Allie's wedding for the world or wished her anything less. Allie was her friend, the next best thing to having a real sister in her life. She deserved the happiness and attention, all of which were a perfect accompaniment to the love she'd found with Mick.

No, for Grace it was more a worry of the unknown than anything else.

A worry borne from seeing Jack again.

She stood at the tall window of one of the upstairs guest rooms in the WCC's main house and watched the beehive of activity taking place on the lawn below. Scores of men and women were working to set up a huge canvas tent and arrange neat rows of white painted chairs beneath. Tables of food would soon follow, and already flowers tucked in long, rectangular boxes sat neatly off to the side of the expansive yard, ready to be arranged in their vases.

The wedding would begin with a prenuptial supper in a few hours' time, but the three giggling women surrounding Jack seemed oblivious to the work needing to be done, appearing far too eager to serve him lemonade and titillate him with their flirting, and it was all Grace could do to stand there and watch it happen.

Yet…she couldn't step away from the window to save her soul, not when the very sight of him filled the emptiness inside her. A heartrending, stomach-twisting yearning to be with him again after so many months apart, to feel those sinewy arms around her and hear his voice, low and husky in her ear.

In the bright afternoon sun, in perfect spring weather, he wore his shirtsleeves rolled up to his elbows and his collar unbuttoned at the throat. With his Levi's snug and his Stetson bumped up on his forehead, his hip cocked and relaxed, merciful saints, he was and always would be the most *masculine* man she'd ever met.

She'd missed him. So much.

She loved him, even more.

Not that he showed an inkling of any love or suffering on *her* behalf at the moment, and emitting a miserable moan, she stepped away from the window and leaned her head back along the wall, papered in pretty yellow flowers.

Her eyes closed. On a weepy sigh, her hands found the gentle swelling on her abdomen.

"Maybe we shouldn't have come back after all, my sweet one," she murmured softly and caressed the little mound of innocence inside her. The precious gift Jack had given her. "We'll only intrude into his new life."

Jack had hired on as Great Falls' newest deputy, she'd learned. Allie spoke of how the police chief made no secret of his pride in having Jack on the force. As his right-hand man, Jack had already proved to be a serious asset against the lawless, and the town's citizens had been quick to show him their gratitude and respect.

"But he deserves to know about us, doesn't he?" Grace insisted, half to herself, half to her baby. "Allie's wedding has given us the perfect opportunity to tell him."

Still, it wouldn't be easy for a man to accept the unexpected responsibility of a child. Her father had been a perfect example of such a man. Carl's, too. Both had been quick to shirk their duties and leave Bess Reilly to raise her children by herself.

Even if Jack did sink so low, Grace was fully prepared to be the best mother she could be. Alone. From the moment she realized she carried a baby in her womb, her whole life shifted from what was important—and what wasn't.

And being a mother was everything Grace wanted to be.

A knock sounded at the door. Her eyes opened, and she straightened from the wall. "Come in."

Allie rushed in, carrying a pink froth of chiffon and silk. "Your gown just arrived from the dressmaker's, Grace. Let's see if it fits now, shall we?"

A new round of guilt assaulted her from all the trouble she'd caused—last minute alterations from a dress too small at the waist.

"Maybe I shouldn't go through with this, Allie. It's not proper etiquette for someone in my condition to be maid of honor, and I don't want to embarrass you—"

"Embarrass me? Pooh!" Allie enveloped her in a quick hug, dress and all. "Who cares about raising a few eyebrows? After what we've both been through?" She stepped back, her happiness shining in her blue eyes. "Besides, you're my dearest friend. I just couldn't get married without you at my side."

No one knew of Grace's expectant state. She'd sworn Allie to secrecy and wouldn't even commit to coming back to Montana until the last minute. Until she had enough nerve…

Allie eyed her knowingly. "You have to tell him, Grace. He'll have your hide if you don't."

She nibbled worriedly on her lower lip. "I know."

"It's not right if he finds out from someone else about his own child. And I think it's absolutely silly you wouldn't let me tell him you were coming. How long do you think you can keep up this charade? Making everyone think I'm having a different maid of honor?"

"Not much longer, I'm afraid." A few hours, at most. Until the prenuptial supper, being set up now, at this very moment.

"I've never known you to be a coward. You'd better tell him, and soon, or I'll do it for you," Allie warned in exasperation.

"I'll tell him. I promise."

Allie's glance fell on the bedside clock. "Oh, my. Look at the time. We have to hurry, Grace. I'll help you try on your dress."

After Grace shimmied into the bridesmaid gown, Allie stepped behind her to fasten the long row of pearl buttons extending from Grace's neck, down her back and to her waist…where no amount of tugging or breath-holding could get the last few to fasten.

Grace groaned. "Now what?"

Allie pursed her lips. "He's going to be big like his daddy, I think."

A knock sounded on the door. "Grace, is Allie in there with you?"

They both turned toward Zurina's voice.

"She is. Come in," Grace called.

The exotically beautiful matriarch of the Wells empire stuck her head in. "I'm sorry to interrupt. The bunting to decorate the tables has arrived, but it's the wrong shade of pink." She halted. Darted her glance between them. "Is everything all right?"

Allie set her hands on her hips. "The dress doesn't fit."

Grace's cheeks flushed. She heaved an embarrassed breath.

"What? It doesn't fit?" Zurina strode into the room, but it only took a single glance at Grace's rounded belly to know why. "Oh. I see."

"You may as well tell her, Grace," Allie said.

"You are going to have a baby," Zurina said, before she could. "No one needs to tell me what I can see with my own eyes."

"Jack's," Grace said, giving up.

"That's wonderful!" Zurina's delight was genuine. "Oh, congratulations! He will make a fine papa!"

"He doesn't know, so mum's the word." Allie's disapproval couldn't be hidden.

"Well, he will soon enough." Zurina replaced her attention for the matter at hand. "Let me see what needs to be done with the dress."

She examined the seam with an efficiency Grace

found relieving. "I can let out a little more fabric. Very easy. Come down to my sewing room, but take the back stairwell so no one sees you. We must keep the surprise. Bring your shoes so we can make sure the hem is just right, too." She rushed toward the door. "You'll look at the bunting, Allie?"

"I'll be right there." Allie headed toward the door after her. "I'll see you soon, Grace. At the supper, if not before."

"Thank you, Allie." Grace vowed to be less trouble from now on.

Alone again, she removed her shoes and hosiery, scooped up the new pair of shoes still in their box and strode in her bare feet to the window to inspect the activity below. Jack was gone, and so were the three females with him, and she hoped they left him alone from now on.

She hastened down the steps toward the small alcove Zurina used as her sewing room. Voices reached her—the animated chatter of women from nearby ranches who crowded the kitchen, chopping and stirring while they prepared mammoth portions of food. In her haste to keep from bothering anyone, but mostly to keep from being seen, Grace emerged from the stairwell and padded quickly toward the alcove, just as Catalin, Zurina's one-year-old daughter, toddled squealing and stiff-legged out of the room, chased by another little girl, and then another, both several years older and enjoying the game as much as the baby.

Grace veered back to avoid them…and careened right into someone walking backward, leading a cart laden with half a dozen glass vases filled to their brims with water. Jack, working in tandem with Trey, and both men veered sideways to avoid hitting Grace and the running children, too.

The cart tilted, despite their scrambling efforts to keep it upright. Several vases clattered to the floor, hurling Grace and the front of her dress with a stunning amount of water. The containers shattered, spraying glass everywhere. Someone screamed. Catalin howled. Grace yelped in horror from being the cause of it all.

"Don't move!" Jack roared.

And though the command rumbled throughout the room, to the very rafters, silencing every voice, every action, it was Grace he speared with a stunned expression.

"You all right?" he barked.

Mortified beyond words, beyond tears, she could only nod, frozen in place by his wrath and her pathetically bare feet, and dripping in the dress that proclaimed her honored place in the wedding. Despairing that they had to meet again, like this.

"She's not bleeding that I can see," Trey said, calmer, giving her a once-over while he scooped up his baby girl for comforting.

"Take Grace upstairs to her room, Jack." Zurina took charge from the alcove doorway. "She's soaked to the skin. Get her out of her dress so it can be dried. I'll send someone up for it shortly. And do be careful with her."

Jack took one step toward her, his boot soles crunching glass...

Grace appealed to Zurina. "I'm so sorry—oh!"

...and swung her up into his arms, halting the rest of the apology Grace intended to make. But Zurina was already busy, combining her efforts with a group of other women to sweep up glass and soak up water off the floor, everyone working quickly to clear the mess so supper preparations could be resumed.

Grace had no other recourse but to hang on to Jack while he hauled her up the stairwell, his jaw set and his anger tangible.

"Which room is yours?" he growled, reaching the hallway.

"The yellow one."

He angled her in effortlessly, sliding her from his arms onto her feet. Her toes sank into the soft square of carpet decorating the floor. He slammed the door shut and glared at her.

"Take the dress off," he said.

Her chin kicked up. "Does it please you to act the barbarian with me?"

A muscle in his cheek moved. He swung away from her, drew in a harsh breath and swung back again.

"What game are you playing, Grace?" he demanded, his voice low. Ominously low.

"What makes you think I am?"

"You all but fall off the face of the earth these past months. Then, you show up like a damned ghost. The day before your best friend's wedding. Her maid of honor." His control seemed on the verge of slipping. "I'm Mick's best man, and *I don't even know you're in the damn wedding party.*"

She didn't move. She couldn't. She knew her plan hadn't been quite perfect, and the regret built inside her, higher and higher, that it wasn't.

"Yes." What else could she say? It was the truth. The cowardly, unfair truth. "I'm sorry."

"How long has Allie known?" he asked, quieter, his control precariously back into place. "Or Zurina?"

"Long enough." She shifted, one bare foot to the other. "Does it matter?"

"You strong-armed them into keeping their mouths shut, didn't you? You forced them to lie for you."

"It wasn't like that."

"The hell it wasn't," he snapped.

She flinched, and the tiny life inside her fluttered within the womb, as if showing his disapproval, too. Reminding her he was there, of all she yet needed to do.

"I told you to take the dress off," Jack said. Softly.

"I can't." Hating her helplessness, she drew in a jagged breath. "The buttons are too small and too hard to reach."

"Come here, then."

He hadn't moved, she noticed. He intended to force her to swallow her pride, to come to him first.

Because he was hurting? As much as she was?

Because he hungered to take her into his arms? As much as she wanted him to?

Because he wanted nothing more than to break down the barriers between them, to unleash the closeness they'd once shared?

Yes. She sensed that about him. All those things. And knew they were true.

She took heart, for knowing gave her courage to tell him what he needed to know.

"We have to talk first," she said.

"Talk?" He narrowed an eye. "All right. How about you start with why it took you so long to come back."

She released her breath. He didn't sound so angry anymore.

"Because you told me you wanted me to be ready, that when I was, I'd know where to find you." Her blood warmed at the memory of where they'd been when he spoke those words. How lusciously warm and naked. Scant hours before she had to leave him. "Even before the train rolled into Minneapolis, I knew I couldn't stay. Not without you. So I worked hard completing my obligations to the Ladies Literary Aid Society. I groomed someone else to take my place as president. I pushed the library plans through. The ground has been broken, and construction started." She hesitated. "I even sold my grandmother's house."

He grunted at that. "And?"

"I have an apartment now. In Paris's building."

"In Great Falls?" He appeared taken aback.

"Yes."

He didn't move. As if he was afraid to believe everything she said. To hope. "I suppose Allie knew all that, too."

"Yes." Grace made no apologies. "So that's why it took me so long to come back. Now, please unbutton me."

She still had one more thing to tell him—the most important thing of all—but she turned, allowing him access to the dress's fastenings. He complied, and in moments, the fabric sagged, and she hastily clutched the mass of chiffon and silk against her chest.

"Might as well take off the chemise, too," he said. "It's soaked along with the dress. You bring a robe with you?"

"Yes." But the time hadn't come to put it on. Yet. "In the armoire."

"I'll get it."

He strode the short distance to the wardrobe with the easy agility so much a part of him. By the time he retrieved the garment and turned back around, Grace had let go of her dress, allowing it to fall into a pink pool at her feet.

She stood boldly in front of him, the thin cotton of her wet chemise clinging to every dip and curve of her body like translucent skin.

"Well, now." His glance slid over her in slow, thorough and very male appreciation. His gray-green eyes smoldered, giving her fair warning of the lust growing steady and strong inside him. "Can't think of a more perfect surprise than what you're giving me right now, Grace, honey."

It took all her control to endure his heated scrutiny.

"A surprise, yes," she said carefully. "But not what you think."

"Yeah?" He came toward her with all the calculated assurance of a man wanting a woman. "Guess you already know what I'm thinking."

He held her robe over one arm. With the other, he reached toward her, as if he intended to pull the chemise off her body, to remove the thinnest of barriers between them....

Until she took his hand and firmly brought it lower, to settle over her belly instead.

"I'm going to have a baby, Jack," she said quietly. "Your baby."

He fell still. And didn't breathe.

For so long.

"A baby?" he choked.

"Yes." She nodded, hardly able to breathe herself. "Early in the fall."

The robe dropped from his arm. "A baby."

"I understand you're a lawman now, Jack," she said, the words picking up speed as they rushed off her tongue. "I don't expect you'll have time for us, what with your new responsibilities and all, but I wanted you to know, and—and I hope you'll find it in your heart to come see us now and again, but if you don't want to, I'll understand that, too, because sometimes men just aren't cut out to be fathers. I'll understand. Truly, I will."

"You think I'll be like my old man?" he growled. "You think I'm going to be another Sam Ketchum?"

"I would certainly hope not," she said firmly. "But—"

"Damn right I wouldn't."

Hope flickered inside her. "It's just that I never knew my own father, or even Carl's, and it wouldn't be too—too foreign to me—"

"Don't compare me to any of them, you hear me?" He clutched her shoulders, as if he itched to shake sense into her, as if it was imperative to convince her of the man he really was. "Because I know what it's like, too, Grace. I know what it means to hurt inside, to bleed and ache so damn bad to have my father love me. I would've done anything so he would."

"Except the love never happens, no matter what we say or do. And then we blame ourselves, when we shouldn't, because it's not our fault. Not at all."

"Yeah." His grip loosened, and raw emotion shimmered in his eyes. "Yeah, that's it exactly."

He trembled, then sank to his knees and spread his hands over the breadth of her abdomen. Gently, tenderly, he pressed a kiss into the rounded softness.

Her throat clogged with emotion, with intense relief

that he actually seemed *happy* about the coming of their child and his determination to have a place in its life. Grace speared her fingers into Jack's burnished gold hair, keeping them there until he rose to his full height and draped the robe around her shoulders. He pulled her against him, snug against his chest.

"I want to be a good father," he said, sounding humbled. "The best a man could be."

"You will be. The best kind of good." She would always know the pain Sam Ketchum brought him. She knew, too, Jack would never wish the same on anyone else's child, let alone his own.

"You'll make a perfect mother, Grace. Nothing like Bess."

Her mouth curved wryly against his shirt. "I hope not."

His arms tightened, as if he never intended to let her leave him again. He sighed into her hair, a contented sound, deep and fervent.

"Are you ready for all this?" he murmured.

"To be a mother?"

"To get married and be a family. The three of us."

"Hmm. There's four, actually."

"Four!"

She laughed. "We can't forget Camille. She'll be a wonderful grandmother to our baby." Thinking of her own grandmother and how much she missed her, Grace drew back and rested her palm across his scarred cheek.

"I liked her from the moment she first brought me a menu, Jack, in Margaret's Eatery."

He chuckled. "She's crazy about you, too, you know. Four of us, it is."

"Until we have more children. As many as we can. Oh, Jack, it's what I want more than anything. To be a real family with you, large or small or something in between."

She slid her arms around his neck and kissed him, long and thorough and rich with the hopes and dreams she held her in her heart. "I love you, Jack. So very much."

Many kisses later, they stood at the window with their arms entwined. But it wasn't the big canvas tent they perused, or the long tables of food and drink, or even the guests beginning to mill about.

Their gazes lingered over the snow-tipped Bear Tooth Mountains in the distance. Lush green grass. And that blue, blue sky.

Montana Territory, as far as she could see.

The beginning of her new life with Jack.

And it promised to be perfect.

* * * * *

COMING NEXT MONTH FROM

HARLEQUIN®
HISTORICAL

Available August 31, 2010

- **HIS DAKOTA CAPTIVE**
  by **Jenna Kernan**
  (Western)

- **CLAIMING THE FORBIDDEN BRIDE**
  by **Gayle Wilson**
  (Regency)
  Book 4 in the *Silk & Scandal* miniseries

- **CHIVALROUS CAPTAIN, REBEL MISTRESS**
  by **Diane Gaston**
  (Regency)

- **SURRENDER TO AN IRISH WARRIOR**
  by **Michelle Willingham**
  (Medieval)
  The MacEgan Brothers

REQUEST YOUR FREE BOOKS!

HARLEQUIN® HISTORICAL:
Where love is timeless

2 FREE NOVELS PLUS 2 FREE GIFTS!

YES! Please send me 2 FREE Harlequin® Historical novels and my 2 FREE gifts (gifts are worth about $10). After receiving them, if I don't wish to receive any more books, I can return the shipping statement marked "cancel." If I don't cancel, I will receive 6 brand-new novels every month and be billed just $4.94 per book in the U.S. or $5.49 per book in Canada. That's a saving of 20% off the cover price! It's quite a bargain! Shipping and handling is just 50¢ per book.* I understand that accepting the 2 free books and gifts places me under no obligation to buy anything. I can always return a shipment and cancel at any time. Even if I never buy another book from Harlequin, the two free books and gifts are mine to keep forever.

246/349 HDN E5L4

Name _____ (PLEASE PRINT) _____

Address _____ Apt. # _____

City _____ State/Prov. _____ Zip/Postal Code _____

Signature (if under 18, a parent or guardian must sign) _____

Mail to the **Harlequin Reader Service:**
IN U.S.A.: P.O. Box 1867, Buffalo, NY 14240-1867
IN CANADA: P.O. Box 609, Fort Erie, Ontario L2A 5X3
Not valid for current subscribers to Harlequin Historical books.

Want to try two free books from another line?
Call 1-800-873-8635 or visit www.morefreebooks.com.

* Terms and prices subject to change without notice. Prices do not include applicable taxes. N.Y. residents add applicable sales tax. Canadian residents will be charged applicable provincial taxes and GST. Offer not valid in Quebec. This offer is limited to one order per household. All orders subject to approval. Credit or debit balances in a customer's account(s) may be offset by any other outstanding balance owed by or to the customer. Please allow 4 to 6 weeks for delivery. Offer available while quantities last.

Your Privacy: Harlequin Books is committed to protecting your privacy. Our Privacy Policy is available online at www.eHarlequin.com or upon request from the Reader Service. From time to time we make our lists of customers available to reputable third parties who may have a product or service of interest to you. If you would prefer we not share your name and address, please check here. ☐

Help us get it right—We strive for accurate, respectful and relevant communications. To clarify or modify your communication preferences, visit us at www.ReaderService.com/consumerschoice.

HH10R

HARLEQUIN®

A Romance

FOR EVERY MOOD™

Spotlight on
— Heart & Home —

Heartwarming romances
where love can happen
right when you least expect it.

See the next page to enjoy a sneak peek
from Harlequin Superromance®,
a Heart and Home series.

*Enjoy a sneak peek at fan favorite Molly O'Keefe's
Harlequin Superromance miniseries,*
THE NOTORIOUS O'NEILLS, *with*
TYLER O'NEILL'S REDEMPTION,
*available September 2010
only from Harlequin Superromance.*

Police chief Juliette Tremblant recognized the shape of the man strolling down the street—in as calm and leisurely fashion as if it were the middle of the day rather than midnight. She slowed her car, convinced her eyes were playing tricks on her. It had been a long time since Tyler O'Neill had been seen in this town.

As she pulled to a stop at the curb, he turned toward her, and her heart about stopped.

"What the hell are you doing here, Tyler?"

"Well, if it isn't Juliette Tremblant." He made his way over to her, then leaned down so he could look her in the eye. He was close enough to touch.

Juliette was not, repeat, *not* going to touch Tyler O'Neill. Not with her fingers. Not with a ten-foot pole. There would be no touching. Which was too bad, since it was the only way she was ever going to convince herself the man standing in front of her—as rumpled and heart-stoppingly handsome now as he'd been at sixteen—was real.

And not a figment of all her furious revenge dreams.

"What are you doing back in Bonne Terre?" she asked.

"The manor is sitting empty," Tyler said and shrugged, as though his arriving out of the blue after ten years was casual. "Seems like someone should be watching over the family home."

"You?" She laughed at the very notion of him being here for any unselfish reason. "Please."

He stared at her for a second, then smiled. Her heart fluttered against her chest—a small mechanical bird powered by that smile.

"You're right." But that cryptic comment was all he offered.

Juliette bit her lip against the other questions.

Why did you go?

Why didn't you write? Call?

What did I do?

But what would be the point? Ten years of silence were all the answer she really needed.

She had sworn off feeling anything for this man long ago. Yet one look at him and all the old hurt and rage resurfaced as though they'd been waiting for the chance. That made her mad.

She put the car in gear, determined not to waste another minute thinking about Tyler O'Neill. "Have a good night, Tyler," she said, liking all the cool "go screw yourself" she managed to fit into those words.

It seems Juliette has an old score to settle with Tyler.
Pick up TYLER O'NEILL'S REDEMPTION
to see how he makes it up to her.
Available September 2010,
only from Harlequin Superromance.

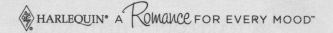

HARLEQUIN® A *Romance* FOR EVERY MOOD™

HARLEQUIN
RECOMMENDED READS
PROGRAM

LOOKING FOR A NEW READ?

**Pick up Michelle Willingham's latest
Harlequin® Historical book**

SURRENDER TO
AN IRISH WARRIOR

Available In September

Here's what readers have to say about this
Harlequin® Historical fan-favorite author

"[T]his book kept me up late into the night…I just had
to find out what happened…I am soooo looking forward
to the next two books Willingham has out."

**—eHarlequin Community Member *Tammys*
on *Her Irish Warrior***

"This was a wonderful story with great characters
and constant twists and turns in the plot that
kept me turning the pages."

**—eHarlequin Community Member *Sandra Hyatt*
on *The Warrior's Touch***

AVAILABLE WHEREVER BOOKS ARE SOLD